"Moving in bright and fast, Apollo caught Rocky flush on the jaw with the stuff champions are made of . . . Rocky dropped low and caught Apollo with a pair of terrific body punches . . . Rocky kept coming, he imagined that Apollo was a frozen side of beef just waiting for Rocky to tenderize its dark flesh . . . but Apollo defrosted like a flash, flicked dread jabs into Rocky's eyes . . . still, Rocky waded in with punches that seemed to bulge out Apollo's back . . ."

Here's your ringside seat for the bloodiest bicentennial in history. The place? Philadelphia. The stakes? The 1976 World Heavyweight Crown. The contenders? Black champ Apollo Creed who spouts poetry at the press and throws dynamite at his opponents . . . and challenger Rocky Balboa—the "Italian Stallion"—a small-time guy with bigtime guts who yearns to be a hero—just once!

ROCKY

PRODUCED BY: Robert Chartoff & Irwin Winkler

EXECUTIVE PRODUCER: Gene Kirkwood

SCREENPLAY BY: Sylvester Stallone

DIRECTED BY: John G. Avildsen

STARRING: Sylvester Stallone as ROCKY

Talia Shire as ADRIAN

Burt Young as PAULIE

Burgess Meredith as MICKEY

Carl Weathers as APOLLO CREED

ROCKY

by
Julia Sorel

Based upon the screenplay
by
Sylvester Stallone

BALLANTINE BOOKS • NEW YORK

ISBN 0-345-25321-3-150

Manufactured in the United States of America

First Edition: December 1976
Third Printing: February 1977

First Special Printing: January 1977
Second Special Printing: January 1977

ROCKY

1

NOVEMBER 12, 1975. A cold night in Philly. Hot action inside the Blue Door Fight Club, a room that resembled a large unemptied trash can. The boxing ring was extra small to ensure constant battle, and the lights overhead had barely enough wattage to illuminate the dim recesses of the mind, much less the dim specters of the ring. Two fighters, one white, the other black, were going at it. The white fighter, Rocky Balboa, had a face covered with scars. His nose was flattened, and his mouthpiece forced his mouth into what looked like a threatening smile. His black hair, shiny with sweat, tickled his eyelids. He moved forward, machinelike, as the black fighter, a younger man, heavy but trim and beautifully muscled, danced around Rocky, banging combinations into his face with great accuracy. Rocky's head jerked back, but the punches didn't even cause him to blink. He grinned at his opponent and kept grinding ahead. The people at ringside sat on folding chairs and clamored for blood. Some of the crowd drank

cheap wine and beer hidden in brown paper bags.
They leaned forward and heckled the fighters:
"C'mon you bums, how about some action . . .
Tear 'is head off . . . Take 'im down for the
count . . ." In the thick smoke everyone was hus-
tling bets. The action in the balcony was even
heavier: Once, in his enthusiasm, a fan had leaned
over too far and fallen over the plain pipe railing,
stealing the show. A housewife, her hair in ex-
quisitely large, round curlers covered with a trans-
parent aqua kerchief, yelled for somebody to
cover a two-dollar bet. A fat man, sweating bullets
and swallowing them, took her on. The bell rang
and the fighters returned to their corners, arriving
there just as somebody heaved a beer can into the
ring. Before the ref could remove it, it lay there
frothing from its triangular metal mouth, a tiny
hollow missile. The black fighter, Spider Rice, spit
something red and thick into a bucket. Later on he
would piss blood, his kidneys on fire from
Rocky's "in the clinch" blows. Spider sneered
across the ring at Rocky.

"I'm gonna bust his head wide open," Spider
hoarsely said to his cornerman.

In Rocky's corner, a shriveled old-timer who
was an employee of the club worked on Rocky
with evident lack of enthusiasm. He pulled the
elastic of Rocky's shorts out from his diaphragm
so that Rocky could take deep, fast breaths: "Ya
waltzin' . . . give the suckers some action."

"Hey . . ." Rocky began, but he was interrupted.

"Ya movin' like a bum. Want some advice . . ."
The old man continued overriding Rocky's objec-
tion.

"Just gimme some water!" Rocky answered, his

mouth dry, his arms hanging at his sides as if he had no elbows and would never bend them again.

A fight fan, sporting a plaid jacket, olive-green shirt, and polka-dot bow tie, rushed up to Rocky. He was about sixty-five, short, weak-looking except for his yellow teeth, which looked as if they could bite right through an elephant's ass.

"Should I bet the fight don't go the distance? Ya feel strong?" the fan questioned.

"Absolutely!" Rocky answered, but he wasn't so sure. One of his eyes was swollen and about to shut, his head was buzzing the flight of the bumble-bee, and his body felt as if it had been reshaped with a meat mallet.

The old man in Rocky's corner was still trying to sell Rocky on some good advice, and Rocky, tired of talking and listening, asked for the mouth-piece. It slid in easily, slippery with spit, and Rocky had his fat but ominous grin back again.

Again the bell clanged, like a trolley coming to the end of its run. Rocky made the sign of the cross, not aware that he was already carrying one, albeit invisible, on his back. The sign of the cross was to protect him, to ask God's help, to create a magical moment of belief in his own invincibility in spite of the odds against him. His opponent made no such sign, but leaped off his stool and made for Rocky, like a hungry bear for its meat. Spider grabbed Rocky in a clinch and deliberately butted him, opening a bleeding cut in the corner of Rocky's eye. Rocky became furious over the foul and drove a flurry of short, tough punches into the man's body. As Spider staggered back-ward, Rocky slammed him on the jaw, and Spider was out for the night—deadsville for him in the raspy, warm, smoke-filled arena; flattened like a paper doll, while the three-dimensional folk swarmed into the ring. The fans loudly went about collecting their bets. The referee didn't even bother to count the loser out—what for, when his recumbent figure was being dragged under the ropes to where he could be placed on a stretcher. The ring was cleared, and two new fighters entered it. Rocky, moving out, tripped on his tattered robe; embroidered clumsily on the back was the hopeful motto: THE ITALIAN STALLION! The announcer finally reported to the crowd: "The winner by a knockout in the third, Rocky Balboa. Next, a six-rounder between two local lightweights . . ."

Without pomp—and who could have had pomp under the circumstance—Rocky climbed out of the ring and bummed a cigarette from a spectator. The fighter on the stretcher passed behind him. He watched for a moment, empty of feeling, then continued up the aisle. Before he even reached the rear of the club, the bell rang, and the next fight began. There were plenty of nerds around who wanted to have their heads handed to them, and an equal number of ambitious comers who were willing to do it for them. Rocky faded into the darkness at the rear of the club.

On the trolley headed back to South Philly, an old woman clucked sympathetically as she studied Rocky's bruised face.

"I'm a fighter," Rocky explained self-consciously.

"My, my. Me-oh-my," the woman said softly, "looks like you the sole survivor of a five-car crash."

"Well, it sure feels that way," Rocky said. "But I'm used to it."

"Wouldn't wanna git used to nothin' like that," she said.

"My face ain't my fortune," Rocky said lightly, to amuse the stranger. "My fists are. I gotta be careful of my fists. When things go right, my fists are beautiful, see . . ."

"Guess you gotta do whut you do," she said, preparing to leave.

"That's it, I'm doin' what I gotta do," Rocky repeated when she was gone. It was a revelation to him, the inevitability of his profession. And the thought made him happy. He relaxed into that place where compulsion and duty having been attended to, a kind of freedom and joy take over.

South Street: empty lots, secondhand stores, boarded-up wooden houses, a kind of shoulder-to-shoulder shantytown where the poor lived and died like link sausages chopped from the mainstream of other link sausages. Rocky didn't notice. It was his neighborhood, and he was blessed with neighborhood insensitivity.

As he walked down the street, Rocky waved at a pair of high-heeled hookers, and they waved back. Even the hookers in the neighborhood dressed like twenty years ago. Manhattan hookers were more stylish in their short shorts, tights, platform shoes, and chubby fur jackets. But style didn't matter to these girls, they just wanted to make a living. Further on he paused in front of the Animal Town Pet Shop. He peered into the dark store and watched a sad, huge dog who was sitting in the window. "Hey, Butkus," he mumbled. The dog didn't budge. Rocky continued to the corner.

Andy's bar. Andy's Italian-American Bar where

Fernet Branca sat on the mirrored shelf nestled between Black Label Scotch, Gilbey's Gin, Isvetskaya Vodka, Fukijo Sake, Jack Daniels Dry Mash, et cetera. Really a house of all nations as far as the liquor went. But the clientele seldom caused one of those bottles to be removed from the shelf; they preferred beer on tap, or maybe a Budweiser, unless someone else was treating.

Rocky entered the bar, which was half-filled with a motley bunch. "Hey, buy me a drink, Rock, don't be a cheap bastard," a drunk pleaded. Rocky smiled and kept right on walking. A woman habitué of the bar, conversing loudly with her cronies (a man who kept his head on the bar right next to his glass, and an old black woman who kept looking at the sport pictures glued to the bar mirror and asking, "Say who is that?"), addressed Rocky as he was passing her and asked: "D'you know how much booze cost me? Not Canadian stuff; regular American booze. Compared to two years ago—makes me sick, I don't even want to think about it. Whatta ya say, bruiser?"

"I say, it ain't the price of booze that makes you sick," Rocky answered, giving her a slap on the ass as he went by.

"Yeah, you make me sick," she retorted.

At the end of the bar, the barkeep Joe Czack and Rocky's friend, Paulie, a stocky man, stood talking.

Joe Czack was a one time club fighter himself who now fought when given the chance. He worked at Andy's Bar at night, and during the day he took a train to Delaware to work eight hours in the Phoenix steelmill. He had laid to rest his dream of ever being a contender years ago.

"Yo!" Rocky greeted them.

"Yo, Rock . . . Look at this face!" Czack said to Paulie. "Where the heck you been? In a gang war?"

"Fightin' . . . you know I been fightin' . . . did good . . . how 'bout two or three beers?" He was dryer than the Sahara Desert. Czack got him the beer and slid them down the bar; they stopped dead in front of Rocky. The way Czack slid drinks down the bar was perfection; he never missed, never spilled a drop.

"Didja win, Rock?" Czack asked.

"Oh, yeah. It was beautiful, a beautiful kayo. Hit 'im with a picture right hook combo . . . Hey, Paulie, ya listenin'?" Rocky shook him by the shoulder, waiting for words of congratulation. Paulie was already juiced and couldn't give Rocky the attention he demanded.

"Yeah, I hear," he managed.

"This tomato musta learned how to fight in China or somethin'. First the pug comes out an' he spits on my chest. Dig it—he *spits* on my chest. Then he keeps movin' an' stickin' with his left, tryin' to thumb my eye out, an' counters with a straight right while his thumb is still hangin' in my eye." Rocky paused to take a long drag of beer. Then he continued, "In the second frame he gets crazy and whips me with his head an' opens this crack here—see this crack—an' all I keep thinkin' about is how bad I wanna smoke an' if I have enough money to get home."

Impatient, Paulie demanded, "How's this terrific story end?"

Joe Czack edging into the conversation, jokingly said, "He marries the prince!"

"I marry the prince an' move upstate forever, right?" Then turning to Paulie, Rocky asked, "Where's ya' sister tonight?" Rocky had a soft spot for Paulie's sister Adrian. She worked in the pet store and had sold Rocky his turtles. She was about as shy as a turtle herself, and plain-looking, but she had something: sensitivity, intelligence.

"I got her home," Paulie replied.

"Every day I drop by an' tell 'er jokes. What she say about me? She ever mention me to you, Paulie?" Rocky inquired.

"Forget 'er. She's too shy—she's been gettin' on my nerves." Paulie let his fingers circle the rim of his glass, "Some people get music when they do this," he said. "I get nothin'."

"I'm gonna drop by tomorrow anyway," Rocky said.

"Yeah, drop by, why not? Yo, I'll see youse later. Got six friggin' tons of beef bein' trucked in tomorrow mornin' at five." Paulie stood up and looked at Rocky's cut eye. "Who you got workin' ya' corner?"

"I don't know, some guy who came with the locker." Rocky shrugged as if to say, I take what I get, that's the way the cookie crumbles.

Paulie, slurring his words but trying to do the friendly thing, managed to say, "I'm glad ya won," before swaying out of the bar.

Czack, wiping the bar where some beer had spilled on its varnished, deep-brown surface, appealed to Rocky on Paulie's behalf. "Why don't ya let 'im work ya' corner again, Rocky?"

Curtly, Rocky replied, "Can't do it."

"So he laid a few bucks against ya." Czack flipped the bar towel over one shoulder and leaned forward, closer to Rocky, in a confidential manner.

"Yo, Paulie is my friend but I can't never forget he bet against me—that really hurts, y'know," Rocky said, fingering a sore spot below one eye.

In front of his house, a two-story structure due to be demolished to make way for a low-cost housing project, Rocky kicked away some litter that had gathered against the steps, and went inside. The narrow hallway had once been painted olive-brown, a proper camouflage for roaches. A single 40-watt bulb illuminated the gloomy corridor. Rocky's one-room apartment was drab, with a stained boxing poster of Rocky Marciano tacked on the wall. Nailed to the far wall was a mattress, its stuffing spilling out of the center, that Rocky used as a punching bag.

Rocky dropped his pea coat on the floor, put on a pair of glasses that were lying on a small cardboard box that doubled as a table, and crossed to the window sill on which sat a small turtle bowl. He lifted one of the creatures and stroked its shell. "Look who's home." Then he began to boil a pan of water on his hot plate. While the water was boiling, he placed an old 45-rpm record on a battered phonograph. The tune was "All in the Game," and Rocky liked it. He picked up a hairbrush and used it like a microphone, miming the record, crooning to imaginary thousands of fans. Between phrases he switched into a bullish fighting stance and threw several punches. After a while, he soaked his badly swollen hands.

2

DAWN. THE JAGGED skyline beginning to glow as the sun rose up behind all the gray buildings, statues, and bridges, emphasizing their pencil-line imprint on the city. The figure of William Penn emerged from the dawn haze, as it sat majestically above City Hall. Rocky walked along the waterfront . . . a band-aid over one eye, hands in pockets . . . wool cap pulled over his forehead. He glanced at the stevedores going about their business, loading and unloading ships' cargoes. He approached a ship being unloaded. Two heavy-set Mafia types were leaning against a parked car. They looked as if they ate tacks for breakfast and washed them down with human blood.

"Yo, Rock. How's your boss?"

"Real good."

"Fightin' again?" the man continued. He began picking his nose.

"Yeah, here and there," Rocky said.

"Maybe we make some money together soon. Give your boss my best," the second car-leaner said. He took out a monogrammed handkerchief and blew his nose. There must have been something in the November air that bothered noses.

Rocky shrugged and moved away. He neared a fat man working a crane. The man looked frightened. He stopped the crane and hurried into the ship's hold. Rocky dashed up the gangplank. Rocky sprinted after him. He lunged and flung the man by the neck against the wall of stacked cargo. Rocky was working his other job now, muscleman for the Mob, extracting money from where no money had been forthcoming.

In terror, the man shielded his face. "Don't hit the face! Not the face!"

"Mr. Gazzo wants the two hundred now!" Rocky hissed.

"Honest to God I'm broke. . . . Gimme a break," the man pleaded.

"I'll give you a break all right! Mr. Gazzo says I should get the two hundred or break the thumb." Rocky was pressing the man against a crate. There was no escape for the jerk.

"Please, I need my hands to work. Christ, don't bust my thumbs." Tears started to trickle down the man's rough cheeks. Suddenly looking around wildly for something to help him, he picked up a large metal hook and threatened Rocky with it, but Rocky remained a rock.

"Goin' fishin'?" Rocky said.

The man dropped the hook.

"What's ya' name again?" Rocky asked.

"Bob," came the swift reply.

"Look, Bob, if you wanna dance, ya' gotta pay the band. If ya borrow, ya gotta pay the man. Me, I ain't emotionally involved. I'm just doin' my job." Rocky's determined expression struck home. The man quickly fumbled through his pockets and handed over a small wad of bills. Rocky counted the money immediately. "A hundred an' thirty. Ya' short!"

"That's it, I'm broke."

"That's it? Completely?"

"That's it." The man began edging away, bounced into an overfull open sack of coffee beans, and the beans poured out, making the floor very slippery indeed.

"What about food and stuff?" Rocky continued.

"You got my food in ya' hand."

Rocky looked almost sympathetically into the man's flushed face. "The juice is climbin' every week."

"I know the juice is climbin' . . . I been workin' six months just to pay the damn interest." The sweat was now pouring off the man, soaking his soft collar, drenching his armpits.

"Ya' still light seventy dollars!" Rocky was getting tired of explaining to the man.

"Hey, what can I say—I ain't got it. Ya' can't squeeze goddamn blood from a stone." The man was becoming cocky.

"Yes I can," Rocky retorted.

"Wait! Be reasonable . . . Be smart. Ya' don't have to break nothin'. Here, take my coat, it's worth fifty or sixty dollars. It's yours." The coat was off and extended to Rocky in a split second. He took it and held it there, undecided, while the man continued to plead his case. "See, why be his flunky? You're a smart guy, Gazzo don't have to know nuthin'. I'll go tape up the hand like ya' broke my thumb, Gazzo won't be wise to nuthin'.

Be a smart guy, keep the coat, we'll fake like ya broke the hand."

Returning the coat, Rocky said, ". . . You should've planned ahead," and walked away.

Later that morning, Rocky sauntered up to his favorite browsing place, the Animal Town Pet Shop, where Adrian Klein, Paulie's sister, worked. She glanced up as Rocky tapped on the window and whistled. Her brown hair was pulled back in a bun, and she had on a pair of granny glasses that made her look older than she was. She managed to smile at Rocky, and he entered the shop.

"How ya feelin' this mornin'? Fulla pep?"

"Fine," Adrian answered.

"How's the turtle food this week?"

"Fine," Adrian said again, very shyly.

In mock annoyance Rocky complained, "Me, I'm kinda aggravated."

"I'm sorry," Adrian said.

"Ain't your fault. Wanna hear this?" Rocky pounded on a pile of pamphlets advertising animal vitamins.

Adrian, though charmed by his vitality and attention, felt slightly intimidated.

"The last food I got here had more moths than flies—an' the moths got caught in my turtle's throat. That makes them cough . . ." Rocky was off to the races, ready to describe in detail his pets' ailments.

The owner of the store, a squat woman of forty, stepped from the back of the shop and waved at Rocky.

"Yo, Gloria. I was talkin' about the turtle food. Like I was sayin' the moths got caught in the turtles' throat an' makes 'em cough"—Rocky coughed, imitating a turtle as best he could—"a little cough, and I had to smack 'em on the shell. An' whatta ya think they got?"

Adrian shrugged.

"Shell-shocked!" Rocky shouted, pleased with his joke.

"Startin' with the bad jokes early today, huh," the owner said.

"Inventin' jokes ain't easy," Rocky confided. He stepped over to a large cage at the rear of the shop. Inside was a huge dog. "How's Butkus today?" he asked.

"Ain't had time to check him out," the owner said.

Rocky opened the cage, and the large dog jumped out and frisked around happily. "Yo, Butkus. Play dead . . . play dead." The dog played dead. Turning to Gloria, Rocky asked, "What kinda dog is this again?"

"Bull mastiff," she answered.

"The owner was supposed to pick him up three weeks ago," Adrian added meekly.

"We're not responsible for animals left over thirty days. We board, it ain't a animal shelter, y'know. Adrian, I want you to clean all those cat cages downstairs, they're a mess."

Adrian nodded, and went downstairs to the basement. Rocky rubbed the dog's coat and followed Adrian with his eyes. He felt deserted. His day was off to a bad start.

Mr. Gazzo and his young bodyguard sat in the front seat of a black Cadillac. Rocky was in the back seat.

"He only had a hundred an' thirty. I think he's good for the rest next week, Mr. Gazzo," Rocky reported.

Patiently, Mr. Gazzo replied, "Sure Rocky, Bob's good for it. That's it for today, kid." He handed Rocky a twenty. "Tomorrow collect from Del Rio. He's late three weeks. How'd ya do last night?"

"Fine."

Gazzo's bodyguard looked at Rocky's bruised face in the mirror and smiled. He hated Rocky. His hate for Rocky made him feel warm all over. "Did ya get the license number?" he asked.

"Of what?" Rocky said.

"Of the truck that run over your fuckin' face." The bodyguard stared at Rocky, challenging him to make something of the remark. Before Rocky could respond, the car veered to the curb in front of Goldmill's Gym.

Cold as ice, the bodyguard said between his teeth, "A meatbag . . . the kid's a meatbag."

"Aw, shaddup!" Mr. Gazzo ordered, "or I'll give ya to the fairies on ya' birthday."

"Hi Rudy, what's up?" Rocky greeted the old Irish man who ran a pretzel stand in front of the gym. Rudy used to be a prize fighter, and now he was blind.

"See the fight last night?" Rudy asked.

"Wah you say? Man, I was fightin' myself." Rocky snatched a pretzel to see whether Rudy could tell he done it. When Rudy didn't mention it, he put the pretzel back.

"Apollo Creed beat the English bum to pieces," Rudy reported.

"Creed's great."

"So what'd ya do last night, Rocky? Didja play 'Rocky-by-baby' and put the bum to sleep?" To Rudy, anyone was a bum who didn't happen to appeal to him. The world was divided into two kinds of people, champs and bums, but even the bums had to be contenders, and the champs had to be vicious, raging maniacs who might eat their victims if they weren't prevented by the rules of the game.

"Yeah, I won. Kayo. Shoulda come down and listen to me fight. Did good!"

"What's that make ya?" Rudy was eager for statistics; without statistics, nothing added up or compared to anything else.

"Forty-four an' twenty—thirty-one kayos," Rocky recited proudly.

"What'd ya use?"

"I used two stale pretzels."

"C'mon, Rock . . . what'd ya use?"

"Right hook combo."

Smiling, Rudy extended his hand and pounded Rocky's arm. "Just what I woulda done. Perfec'."

"Ain't nobody called me perfec' since I was a baby," Rocky said, dropping a coin in the paper cup on the stand.

"Maybe you only been perfec' twice," Rudy guessed.

"Hey!" Rocky flipped another coin on top of the one he had just sent into the cup. "Gotta have one of these pretzels! The Italian Stallion trains on pretzels so he won't get all twisted like a pretzel."

Goldmill's Gym was nearly full. The measured beat of skip ropes and the throbbing dat-dat-dat-

dat-data-data-dat of the speed bags made the room
come alive. Music by the Isley Brothers blared out
over the loudspeakers, adding background to the
clang of the automatic timers, the snorting and
heavy breathing of fighters, and the thudding of
heavy bags. The room was fifty per cent black,
thirty-five per cent Latin, ten per cent white, and
five per cent of indeterminate but aggressive ori-
gin.

As Rocky walked though the gym, many of the
fighters yelled greetings; they were aware of his
bout the other night:

"Hey, hear ya knocked Spider Rice out in the
sixth?"

"The third. Shoulda seen it," Rocky responded.

As Rocky passed another fighter punching the
heavy bag, the fighter removed his glove and said,
"Hey, Rock, touch my hand."

"How come?"

"C'mon, it's important," the fighter insisted.

Rocky touched the fighter's bare hand gingerly,
"Feels like a hand."

"Can ya tell I just whacked off?"

Rocky smiled and moved away; he wished he
had thought of it first. Then he wondered whether
the guy really had just beat his meat and not
washed his hand. "Naw," he decided, "naw—
that'd be vulgar."

On the dressing room wall was a sign that read
NO KISSING, an easy rule to follow. Rocky got to his
locker, tried to open it, and failed. He leaned his
ear against the lock and rolled the tumblers. No
go. He shook the thing and tried to pry it open with
no luck. It was puzzlement time. Rocky sat on the
bench to ponder the situation a bit. After a second

or two of deep thought, Rocky stood, seized the bench, and smashed the lock open. Opening the door, he was startled to see a set of very flashy threads. "These ain't my clothes," Rocky mumbled. Rocky saw a picture of several black girls pasted to the door. "These ain't my pictures," Rocky said softly, an ugly thought dawning on him.

A short, powerful man of thirty-five meandered into the gray environs of the locker room. His head looked as if it had sprouted thick brown wires, standing straight up, that had been shaped with hedge clippers.

"Yo, Mike. What's happened here?" a bothered Rocky asked.

"It ain't your locker no more, Rock. Boss got a bug up his ass. Don't know what."

"Whatta ya talkin' about it ain't my locker no more? I'm a member, I even decorated it myself, an' sprayed the inside wit roach spray. Went through a lot of trouble to keep it ship shape."

"Listen, I'm with you. But I don't own the place, right? Ya gotta talk to Mickey. Mickey's the one." He reached under the bench and came up with the curled picture Rocky had decorated his locker with. "I think this's yours, Rocky."

Confused, Rocky followed Mike across the room. Mike leaned his head into the shower room. Two Latin fighters were lathering up. One was a featherweight, the other just big and sloppy, on his way to becoming an unsightly heavyweight.

"Hey, Peanut, gimme some soap, man," the big one said to Mike. Obviously he was new and totally unaware of Mike's status at the gym.

Mike, sore as hell, yelled, "Hey, nobody, but *nobody,* calls me Peanut—especially you, chico!"

The fat Latin repeated what he had just said without batting an eyelid, only he said it louder this time. "Peanut . . . hey you, *Peanut,* gimme some soap."

Both fighters, dancing in the warm shower, began to laugh. It was great fun getting Mr. Peanut hopping mad, or so they thought; but Mike was furious. He removed a bar of soap from his pocket and hurled it at the insulting fighter. It hit just above the man's head. The fighters were shocked into silence. Mike turned and exited with Rocky, the fighter's loud curses following them.

"You were ready to bite that guy's face," Rocky said admiringly.

"Lip service I don't take from nobody," Mike said.

"You're someone to watch out for. You sure are a dangerous guy today." Rocky complimented Mike with a smile, who faked a friendly punch at Rocky and hurried off to do some gym chore.

Near the entrance, on a stool, sat Mickey Goldmill, entrepreneur, in his late seventies, resembling a latter-day George Raft. Having been around so long, there was no one he respected and no one who could pique his interest. He was bored.

"Hey, how ya feelin'?" Rocky asked him.

"What?" Mickey pretended instant deafness.

"I said, how ya feelin'?"

"You a doctor?" Mickey turned away from Rocky. How should he feel—one foot in the grave, the other in a Dr. Scholl's footbath.

"Ya got troubles today?" Rocky said softly. He was trying to lead into the question of his locker and trying not to be too angry with the old man.

Not giving an inch, and just as mean as before,

Mickey spit in the corner and wiped his mouth with the back of his hand. "Don't worry about my problem. What's *your* problem?"

"I was talkin' with ya' man, Mike, and he . . . hey, how come I been put outta my locker?"

Without ceremony the old man said, "Dipper needed it."

Rocky turned and looked at Dipper sparring. Dipper was young, a muscular heavyweight with a mean expression.

Mickey continued, scathingly, "Dipper's a contender. You, you're a tomato."

"Tomato?"

"Dipper's a climber. You're a tomato. Facts is facts. I run a business."

Rocky, to keep from sinking to his knees and begging the old man to call him anything but a tomato, fastened on the lively sight of a young middleweight time-skipping as his trainer sang "Fascinatin' Rhythm."

The old man was wound up and spinning; he just had to knock Rocky down. He did it in the guise of good advice. "Look, do yaself a favor, retire. How old are ya, kid?"

"What?" Rocky asked as if he had not heard what he heard.

"How old?"

"Come July I'm twenty-five," Rocky lied.

"More like thirty!" Mickey insisted.

"Twenty-five, thirty . . . what's the difference? It took me two months to learn the combination of that locker."

"Ya' legs must be goin'," Mickey stated. "There ain't no paraplegic contests for fighters; ya can't turn the wheels with gloves on."

"Yeah, they're goin', so are yours. That's nature. That was my locker for six years." He couldn't put a dent in the old man's armor because it was made of reality, it stood up and shone like the truth. But it was hard for Rocky to face the facts.

"Fight last night? Ya win?" Mickey inquired, hoping to bring home his truth more strongly.

"Yeah—kayo." Rocky was almost sorry to admit to winning.

"Who did you fight?"

"Spider Rice!"

The news made the old man cheerful. "Rice is a bum."

"You think everybody I fight is a bum." The old man reminded him of his father, always critical, always tearing him down . . . but his father was dead, and there he was thinking of him in the present.

"Ain't they?" Mickey shot Rocky a quick, indifferent look and removed a rosary from his pocket, then idly rolled it around his fingers. "Ya want the truth . . . ya got heart, but ya fight like an ape. All ya got goin' is a straight nose. Ever think about retirin'?"

Rocky didn't know what Mickey meant about his nose—it had been punched so often that the bridge was sway-backed and the pug was as puggy as a nose could get . . . and the part about retiring— what would he retire to? "No, I ain't never thought 'bout retirin'," he answered.

"Think about it," Mickey said with all the weight of an oracle. "Give it some thought."

Shrugging, Rocky moved away. Damn, he wasn't going to think about it; just because some tired old fart told him it was all over didn't mean it was—fate could change things, and sometimes did. However, fate couldn't get him his old locker back; only the old fart could—it was his gym.

When Rocky was out of earshot, Mickey leaned over to Mike and, gesturing toward Rocky, said, "Known him since he was fifteen. A waste of life."

Dejected, Rocky traveled to the locker room once more. He passed Big Dipper, who was sparring in the ring. Dipper spit a mouthful of water into a bucket and looked smugly at Rocky. "I dig yo' locker, man."

Wordlessly, Rocky moved on.

Sunset. The light died, or played dead, like Butkus the dog. A close observer might have noticed the light quiver as it rested at the foot of South Street, but there were no close observers. Even Rocky's attention was elsewhere, actually fastened on the last piece of chicken he was eating out of a bag. When he got to the pet shop, he tapped on the window with a bone. Inside, Adrian was arranging pet toys on the counter: rubber bones, balls full of catnip, a mirror and bell for the birds, a single slipper for the puppy who likes to eat slipper. Adrian saw Rocky and tensed. She had been hoping to see him, but when she did, a part of her became terrified. She could not express what she felt about him; it wasn't only sexual attraction, but a kind of acknowledgment that they were the same kind of people: lonely, shy, and caring.

"Good night to catch pneumonia," Rocky said. The weather was always a nice, neutral opener.

Adrian did not answer, but smiling slightly moved behind the counter.

"Ah . . . I came in here for somethin'," Rocky began. "Oh, yeah, would ya like somebody to walk ya home?"

Adrian wanted to say yes, but she couldn't say it—a tremendous inferiority complex didn't permit it. Instead she squeezed the empty rubber sides of the toy mouse again until it squeaked piteously.

"Whut's the mouse sayin'?" Rocky asked.

Adrian blushed and shrugged her shoulders.

Understanding her embarrassment, Rocky changed the subject. "Hey, how's my buddy doin'?" He looked into Butkus's cage. "Nice dog. Well, I'll see ya later."

"Good night Rocky." Adrian watched his departure with mixed emotions.

A short while later, Rocky arrived at Andy's bar. Out of deference to Andy, he disposed of his Colonel Sanders bag of bones before entering. Immediately, Joe Czack set a mug of beer in front of him and rubbed his scarred eyes. Rocky seemed anxious. He was looking for Paulie.

"Seen Paulie?"

"He was complainin' about havin' sore joints an' then went into the can to comb his hair about an hour ago." Automatically, Czack replaced the mug of beer that Rocky had quaffed in one motion. Rocky left the second beer, and crossed the room to the rest room.

It was a vile stench hole, overwhelming to any who happened to be sober. Essence of vomit clung to the walls, and crystallized yellow violets of urine lined the floor around the toilet bowl. A desensitized Paulie was trying to comb his hair in front of the only piece of mirror in the room. He was not pleased with what he saw in the mirror.

"Yo, Paulie," Rocky greeted his friend.

Paulie wavered in front of the mirror fragment, as if the greeting had greatly struck him. He swayed drunkenly, losing his reflection for an instant. "Yo, Rocky. Look at this mirror. I'd like to kill the friggin' moron who broke this mirror. Hey, man, look, I got half a face. Whut happen to the other half?"

"Mus' be playin' aroun'. It'll be back." He straightened Paulie in front of the mirror. "There it is, that's all there is, the whole face: left side, right side. Yo, Paulie."

"What?" Paulie asked, touching his forehead and the bridge of his nose. "I got a interesting face," he said.

"Your sister's giving me the cold shoulder," Rocky explained. "But I think she digs me."

"Ignore her," Paulie said coldly, still admiring his face, combing his hair a different way. "You could do better than my sister."

"Ya see, every morning and every night I pass by ya' sister's shop, I smile, I tell 'er jokes . . . but nothin', she looks right through me. What am I— made of glass?"

"Looks right through ya, huh?" Paulie's mouth twitched.

"Yeah, an' sometimes she looks at me like I was a plate of greasy leftovers. Somethin' wrong with my face? Whatta I need, a nose job to connect with ya' sister?"

"Ya wanna know what I think, huh? My sister's a friggin' loser."

Rocky was taken aback. He didn't expect Paulie to react that way. "Hey . . . hold on . . ."

"Sometimes she gets me so crazy I'd like to split her eyes with a razor."

Rocky moved toward the door. "Don't get mental, man."

"Ya caught me in a bad mood." Paulie put his comb into his jacket.

"Ya' alway's in a bad mood."

"Adrian ain't sharp," Paulie continued.

"But you are, right?" The rest-room stench became overwhelming; Rocky covered his nose with the neck-line of his T-shirt.

"Yeah. She's a loser. She don't do nothin'. She don't enjoy life. She reads . . . brainy. She's too shy to get along in this world, y'know. Pushin' thirty friggin' years old. She's gonna die alone if she don't wise up."

"I'm thirty myself," Rocky acknowledged sadly.

"An' you're dying alone, too," Paulie added.

"I don't see no crowd around you neither."

Paulie didn't want to talk about himself; he figured he didn't have a chance anyway. But his sister . . . that was different. Then, pointing at the wall, letting loose some of his anger, he yelled, "I wanna kill the friggin' moron who broke the mirror."

Rocky guided Paulie through the narrow rest-room door. Though stumbling, Paulie managed to continue talking, "My mother had 'er under her thumb. Y'know—my ol' lady ate up her personality, was afraid she'd leave her, tol' her horrible stories of whut could happen to a girl who kissed a guy widdout marryin' him."

"An' now she's afraid of men?" Rocky asked.

"Yeah, mebbe. She's afraid of somethin'."

Rocky hesitated before he made this suggestion—he knew it was a touchy subject—but still,
Paulie was his friend, and he owed it to friendship
to speak his mind. "Do ya feel she might need the
help of a . . . I don't know, maybe a shrink?"

Paulie went wild and bellowed, "She ain't sick!"
He stood roaring drunk in the center of the room.
Everyone's attention was riveted on him. "Sick
don't run in the family! She's shy, man, that's all,
shy!"

Rocky, embarrassed and very self-conscious,
stared at the floor. Speaking low, he said, "What
can I say?"

Paulie, still bellowing, gave his captive audience
the lowdown on his sister, "The girl's dryin' up. I
feel responsible, man. She's gotta live a little before her body rots! You're a pal, Rock—how
'bout yo' talk to her. It's Thanksgivin'."

To calm him down, Rocky said, "Sure."

"Tomorrow you come for some Thanksgivin'
dinner, right?"

"Absolutely," Rocky agreed.

At last Paulie smiled, and Rocky guided him to
a booth. He sank down, slumped in the corner,
and closed his eyes. Rocky stepped to the bar.
Andy the owner and sometimes bartender spoke to
him confidentially. "That was a lotta crap to go
through for a dinner invite." Rocky nodded and
raised his eyes toward a suspended television; the
nightly sports broadcast was on. The sports commentator was at the airport and about to interview
the heavyweight champion of the world, Apollo
Creed. Creed was twenty-eight years old, tall,
smooth-muscled, black, with barely a scar on his

light coffee-colored face. He was followed by an entourage of mixed trainers and cornermen. Also tagging along was a small group of hangers-on.

The commentator, pushing his microphone close to Creed's face, asked, "How was the fight, champ?"

Apollo looked at the plane and answered with a flashy smile, "Very high an' very fast." Apollo's crowd smiled almost automatically, and there were murmurs of "Right on."

"Apollo, how would you rate this last British challenger, Henry Wilcoxson?" the commentator asked. Canteen trucks had pulled up to the plane behind the champ, and food began being loaded on.

"He was big, an' very nasty, so I destroyed him in a hurry. Now I'm gettin' ready for Lee Green next month." The champ put on a very serious face.

"You're referring to the much-publicized bi-centennial fight?" The camera closed in on a tiny red, white, and blue flag the champ had pinned to his lapel.

"That's right. It's gonna be the greatest sportin' event in this country's history. A gala occurrence." Apollo Creed reached back to where a tall young woman was standing and drew her forward to stand next to him. She was pretty enough to be a model. "This is Miss Betty Palmer, she's mah personal and official biographer. Takes down everythin' I say for posterity, don' you, Miss Betty? Show the folks youah notebook." The pretty woman took a stenographer's notebook out of her classy lizard bag and waved it in the air. The hangers-on grinned and pinched each other. Imagine calling his newest lady a biographer—that really grabbed them.

The commentator continued to question the champ, asking questions dyed-in-the-wool fans wanted to know. "Is the fight still to be held in Philadelphia, Apollo?"

Apollo, now in a rush to get on board the airliner, answered quickly, "The Bicentennial Heavyweight Championship of the World is gonna be held in Philadelphia, the nation's cradle. It's gonna be a fight like none that's been seen."

"Where you off to now?"

"Goin' home 'cause I miss my children an' can't go no more time without seein' them." Apollo Creed was walking slowly backward, led by two of his friends. The young lady "biographer" waited respectfully on the sidelines. Obviously she was not going home with the champ. Home was where the champ's wife was, and what he said to her was not for posterity.

"Any advice for young boxing hopefuls?" the interviewer asked, as if advice would help a young hopeful become champ.

Apollo looked straight into the camera, giving it the triple whammy, hexing it, attempting to hypnotize the thousands of people watching. "Stay in school an' use your brains, dig? Be a lawyer, be a doctor. Carry a leather briefcase. Forget about sports! Sports make ya grunt an' smell. Be a *thinker,* not a stinker!" Apollo's entourage laughed and moved on.

Alone, facing the camera, the commentator closed, "Larry Carrol at Kennedy Airport with the champion, Apollo Creed."

Rocky continued to stare at the TV with a pensive expression long after the sports show had cut away. Andy the bartender was remarking on the state of affairs in the world, which wasn't too pleasant. "Nobody cares what's happenin' in the world of sports any more. Downhill. Baseball, downhill, basketball downhill. Football's goin', too. Bank on it."

A drunk, aiming for accuracy, almost hit the mark with, "Baseball used to be America's one sport . . ."

Andy cut in, "Sure . . . nuttin' like squattin' through a great double-header, but now baseball's all business." Andy took a drink and continued, "Where are the real fighters? The pros. Today we dig clowns."

"Whatta ya sayin', Andy? The man's a champ," Joe Czack said.

Andy wouldn't be moved. He liked his fighters serious. "Creed's a clown. Clear those tables."

Rocky came out of his momentary daze and said, "Hey."

"What?" Andy replied.

"He took his best shot an' became champ. What shot did you ever take?"

"Yo, Rock, you ain't happy with yourself? Nice. But me, I gotta business here. I don't need to take no shot."

Despondent, Rocky got up and walked over to Paulie, who was dead to the world in the booth. Seeing that he was out cold, Rocky turned toward the door and went out.

"Take a shot he says! Sure I'll take a fuckin' shot!" Andy said and poured a shot.

Out in the cold, lonely, blue-gray night, Rocky went past the all-night sandwich shop that had a beautiful red, orange, and yellow neon sign in its window, ATOMIC HOAGIE SHOP. The hoagie itself was shaped like a spaceship, brilliant neon straws exploding below it as if the entire sandwich were about to be launched into space (or space in someone's mouth). Out front, were several young people, on stage as it were, in the brilliant light. They were much too young to be out so late. A boy with a badly chipped tooth beckoned to Rocky, "Yo, Rocks, buy us some wine, man."

"No wine, kid, bad for ya brain," Rocky said.

The kid insisted aggressively. "C'mon, man, it's cold outside."

"No wine," Rocky repeated.

Then, even more snotty than before, chipped tooth put the touch on Rocky for a dollar. "S'only a dollar. You can afford it."

"Why?" Rocky asked, curious as to what the kid would say.

Sarcastically, chipped tooth said, " 'Cause we dig you, man. Gimme a dollar."

Rocky, wondering where the kid got the gall to pick on him, calmly said, "No dollar."

Chipped tooth turned to his friend and asked, "Hey, give Rocky a dime."

"How come?" his friend inquired.

"So he can call all his friends," chipped tooth laughed.

Rocky, mildly embarrassed, said, "That's an old one."

Chipped tooth came up real close and leaned on Rocky, the way a salesman of porno pictures in a foreign land might, and wheedled, "Buy us some Thunderbird, man."

Rocky ignored the statement and faced a very young girl, of about eleven or twelve. She was leaning against the wall, holding it up like a French whore, and smoking like a tepee.

"Is that Marie? Marie, ya' brother know ya' hangin' out so late?" Rocky asked. He felt tenderness toward her, she looked so little and so tough at the same time. She had on a pair of overalls, workmen's boots, a torn secondhand man's jacket, and her hair was tucked into a straw Panama hat.

The girl pretended indifference, attempting to impress her friends. "Fuck you!" she hollered.

Rocky was amazed at the vulgarity. She was only a kid. "What'd you say?" he asked.

"Fuck you, yoyo," she obliged him, with an added hooker's description. Yeah, he was a yoyo, connected to life by a string, going up, going down, till one day he would hang there slack, and even the proper winding wouldn't put the life back in him. The gang mocked Rocky, laughing aloud at his chagrin.

Angered and shocked, Rocky grabbed her arm. It was attached to the rest of her, so she came along. "Did these guys teach you to talk dirty? Huh?"

"Hey . . ."

"What?"

"Eat shit, man!" She had street smarts and was strutting her stuff. All eyes were on her.

When it came to kids using "bad" language, Rocky was a puritan. He believed the next step was white slavery, and after that a stiff sentence in purgatory. "Don't you ever say that," then turning to the gang, he warned them, "You guys talk like that in front of a little girl . . . you guys are scum!"

"This is our place, dig," chipped tooth said. But he and his friends backed up.

"Don't ya never come round this girl. Go home." Rocky, his voice hard and cold, meant business.

But some kids are stupid, they have to prove themselves in spite of insane odds. Another runt declared the corner *his* corner and told Rocky to go. Rocky moved forward, and they scattered.

As chipped tooth back-pedaled, he warned Rocky, "We'll kill you, man. We gotta gun."

"Pull heat on me? I'll dent ya' face." Rocky led the girl away. He decided to walk her home. They cut through a dark schoolyard, passing through the beams of light cast by weak floodlights located at the top of the school building. The atmosphere was eerie. And the combination of huge, heavyweight Rocky Balboa, guiding the tiny girl Marie, was the reverse of a tugboat helping a giant ocean liner into safe harbor. If he went in too deep, Rocky might not be able to get out. The girl was not as sweet and innocent as he supposed. "How come ya wanna hang out with those guys? They teach ya bad things."

"I like 'em," Marie said indignantly. "If you don't, you can fuck yourself." She shook her head angrily, and her hat fell off.

"Hey, when I was your age, there was only one girl who talked like that in the whole neighborhood."

"Yeah?" Marie was bored. She attempted to light a cigarette. Rocky nonchalantly tossed it to the ground. "That costs money. What gives you the right to toss away my personal property?" she challenged.

"Make your teeth yella," Rocky warned, adapting a lighter tone.

"I like yella teeth!" she sassed right back.

"Makes your breath like garbage."

"Maybe I like garbage," Marie said, only not in so assured a manner as she had declared her liking for yellow teeth.

"Nobody likes garbage. Rats like garbage, that's who . . . Anyway, this girl from my neighborhood, the girl with the dirty mouth, wasn't bad-lookin', like you, but the guys wouldn't take her out for any serious datin'." Rocky felt like he was Marie's father and he had to straighten her out.

"Why wouldn't anyone date her seriously?" Marie felt as if she were talking to a foreigner who was describing the natives of his land. She listened to him as to a story, but didn't relate to what he was saying in any way.

" 'Cause that's the way guys are. They laugh when ya talk dirty. They think ya' cute for a while, but then ya get a reputation, an' watch out. Nobody's ever gonna take ya serious. Ya get no respect. I gotta use a bad word—whore. You'll end up becomin' a whore."

"C'mon, Rocky, I'm twelve. Besides, don't Joe Namath have a reputation, and he ain't no whore."

"That's a different kinda reputation. He didn't get it by bein' no smart-ass, he worked hard an' kept his nose clean and he respected hisself."

Rocky found that he was talking to himself. Marie didn't have a clue to what he meant. At her

age, all she wanted was some attention, but she
might get more than she bargained for. "How old
you are doesn't matter. You don't really have to
be a whore, just act like one, an' that's it," he
warned her.

"Bullshit," Marie offered.

Rocky had the urge to slap Marie but that
would have been awful: taking her home to protect her, and then slamming her. He bit his lip
and continued, "Yo, ya' lookin' at it from a weird
viewpoint. Ya gotta be realistic—if ya get a bad
rep, twenty years from now people will say, 'Do
you remember Marie?' 'No, who was she?' 'She
was that little whore who hung out at the Atomic
Hoagie Shop.' 'Oh, now I remember!' See, they'll
remember the rep."

Rocky and Marie left the dark schoolyard.
Standing in the shadows of the building were three
young muggers. The light from their cigarettes
flared red in their faces. When Rocky and Marie
walked up the block, the muggers followed
them. Rocky, aware of this, turned and faced
them. They paused, studied him from a distance
of twenty yards. Rocky gave a loud boxer's snort,
wiped his nose with the side of his thumb, and
rolled his shoulders. The muggers became intimidated, slowly peeled off, and meandered away.
Rocky turned to Marie, who had been standing
behind him. He pointed down the block. "That's
your house, ain't it?"

Marie nodded.

"Listen, I hope ya don't . . ."

"I won't," Marie answered.

"What was I gonna say?" Rocky queried.

"Ya hope I don't keep actin' like a whore or I'll turn into one, right?" Marie guessed.

"Yeah, somethin' like that," Rocky agreed. He felt he had made some impact on her life. They exchanged smiles, and Marie moved away.

"Hey, Rocky."

"Yo?"

"Fuck you, motherfucker!" She ran into her house as Rocky looked on in dismay.

As Rocky walked off, he put himself down; the girl had made an impression on him. Yeah, he thought, who're you to give advice?

3

It was part of Miles Jergens' character to believe every calamity a blessing in disguise. Armed with this philosophy, he could afford to smile, even when everyone else wore scowls and bemoaned their fate. However, fate had dealt this successful promoter a difficult quandary to get out of. A meeting was held at his opulent office in the Franklin complex, with Apollo Creed, and Apollo's lawyer and trainer. Floor-to-ceiling windows let the light drench walls, ceiling, and floor alike with glaring brilliance. It was a cold but sunny day. Jergens had his secretary draw the blinds so that he wouldn't have to squint at the papers before him. Creed was sitting back, his eyes closed, listening carefully and thinking.

"Are the doctor's reports confirmed?" Creed's lawyer asked.

Jergens answered, "Definitely," then, reviewing the paper in front of him, said, "It says here Mac

Lee Green has suffered a seriously cracked third metacarpal in his left hand."

Skeptically, the lawyer repeated the previous question, "Did you say that report was *definitely* comfirmed?"

"That's right, Mr. Sawyer," Jergens said. He glanced at Creed to see whether he had anything to say. Creed remained impassive.

"Isn't it your responsibility to supervise . . ." the lawyer began. He tapped nervously on his attaché case.

Jergens cut in, "Apollo, I suppose we could cancel the fight if you only want to fight Green." He didn't want to antagonize Creed, the world champ; he wanted to assuage him if he could. But Apollo Creed wasn't ready to say anything yet. It was all simmering, all the ideas would come together before long. He let the others discuss the matter at hand.

Mr. James, Apollo's trainer, and personal friend, said, "It ain't just Green. What about the time Apollo put in? He oughta fight you."

Jergens winced at the image of Creed laying one on him. He wouldn't live to read about it in the papers. Mr. Sawyer explained what the trainer had meant. "What Mr. James is saying is, what compensation is morally due Mr. Creed for time invested in prefight promotion."

When it came to money, Jergens was on sure grounds. "I believe we can find a solution," he promised. "Anyone like a piece of teaberry gum?" He had just found a pack in his desk drawer. He realized how odd a question it was, if there were no confirmed gum chewers in the group. Luckily Creed himself took a stick.

"Solution, Mr. Jergens," the lawyer continued, "the only solution is that you had better find another ranked contender in a hurry."

Jergens tightened on the spot. His knuckles under his desk whitened, his teeth ground together, and a nervous tic under his eye reappeared. He hadn't felt like this since the death of his pet parakeet. "I contacted Ernie Roman. He's fighting in France the same week," he said.

"Then give us Buddy Shaw. He's ranked fifth. Apollo'll carry 'im for a couple rounds," the trainer suggested.

"Shaw's fighting in South America. Why not just postpone the bout until July Fourth?" Jergens asked, knowing full well that Apollo's people would immediately think of a good reason why not. He tore open a package of Tums and popped a few. "Huh, why not? Think of it: July the Fourth, Roman candles, sparklers, all kinda fireworks, and the brightest fireworks of all—Apollo Creed's fight to protect the championship!"

"Hell with the Fourth of July!" the lawyer shouted. "Ten thousand things'll be occurring on the Fourth of July. Apollo wants to be first!"

The trainer, his voice as loud as the lawyer's, came on with a dud of a suggestion, "What about that sucker, Billy Dukes?"

Disgustedly, Jergens looked at him, then said in a voice of quiet desperation, "Developed a bleeding ulcer and retired. Look, I know my business, I wasn't born yesterday. I've called every worthwhile goddamn contender, but they say five weeks is not enough time to get into shape."

"Shape nothin'," the trainer said, "they're scared; they don't wanna be whipped in front of one billion people. They don't wanna be dissected on the country's birthday." He cut the air with his hands, dissecting it with precise crisscross movements resembling karate more than boxing. A typical trainer, he was awfully out of shape himself: he was fat, his avoirdupois protruding from a baggy sweatshirt, and his face was a spongy half-moon, hanging above a double chin. He had a nice smile when it wasn't being invaded by a cigar.

Jergens said, "You don't say so!"

"I do say so!" the trainer emphasized. "In fact, I just said so."

Mr. Sawyer, who had been listening with amusement, suddenly sat bolt upright. A lightning idea had struck him and traveled from his spine to his skull, where the idea machinery seldom lay dormant. "Hey, relax. Maybe what this fight needs is a novelty." He sat back and polished his star-sapphire ring by rubbing it with an elaborately monogrammed handkerchief.

"Novelty? You mean like some freak show? Ya want Creed to fight with a midget and get broken knees? Ya want him to get in the ring with a lady boxer and get a bust in the mouth?" Jergens laughed obscenely at the burlesque skit evolving in his mind. If he listened to Creed's people he'd be promoting in a flea circus, not in one of the biggest arena's in the country.

Mr. Sawyer refused to break the tension. He didn't laugh. He was serious. While he spoke to Jergens, he adjusted the crease in his trousers but never took his eyes off Jergens. "No, I don't conceive of something freakish; rather something unusual . . . bizarre . . . to draw the crowd in."

"Sure, promise them a murder, they'll buy tickets,

but I promote fights, sporting events, not side shows." Jergens loosened his collar, unbuttoned his plaid jacket, rolled his chair back till it touched the wall, then lifted his feet onto his desk.

Ominously, the lawyer said, "You'll promote what we want!"

"I promote for Apollo, not you," Jergens asserted.

"As his attorney, I speak for Apollo!"

Apollo slammed his hands on the sides of the chair and stood up. Behind him, a map of the world covered an entire wall. He seemed to have been thrust out of three continents into the room. He looked like a god, and sounded like one, as he boomed, "Nobody speaks for me! My voice is the voice of brightness. My thought is the thought of rightness "

Everyone froze. Flash cryogenics. Instant ice pops.

Apollo continued. He didn't aim to bring a summer thaw just yet. He had put them in deepfreeze, and there they'd stay—for a while. "Now I talk. Maybe you're right about this fight needin' somethin' different, but you're jivin' like fools. Now here's what's goin' down. On January first, the first day of the bicentennial, I'm gonna fight me a local poor underdog, dig? A snow-white underdog. An' people are sentimental, man, they'd like nothin' better than Apollo Creed lettin' some unknown get a shot at the greatest title in the world on this country's birthday. Now that's the way I want it!" Apollo turned toward the door and opened it.

"It's very American," Jergens said.

Apollo swiveled and shook his head, "No, man, it's very smart." The trainer and attorney followed him out without so much as a sidelong glance at Jergens, who was left mumbling into his arm, on which he had placed his weary brow.

Late that afternoon, Mr. Gazzo's white 1970 Cadillac pulled up to Rocky's apartment. Rocky was in the back seat with the loan shark. Gazzo's bodyguard was driving. Gazzo was flipping through a small black notebook.

"Matter of fact," Gazzo ordered, "Next Wednesday, grab a grand from Snyder."

"Snyder, right," Rocky said.

"An' Thursday, two yards from Cappoli, okay?" Gazzo continued, going down the short list.

"Okay," Rocky agreed. "Cappoli, the junk man. I bought a nice lamp from him once, cheap, still got it."

"That's nice, Rocky," Gazzo responded. "I'm glad you got a nice lamp 'cause you shouldn't strain your eyes, not if you wanna spend a lotta time lookin' at this nice girl I hear you're goin' out with tonight."

"How'd you know?" Rocky asked, embarrassed.

"You think I don't hear things?" Gazzo smiled.

"Paulie's sister," Rocky admitted.

The bodyguard twisted his neck around so that Rocky could catch the full disdain of his expression. "I hear she's retarded," he sneered.

"She ain't retarded, she's shy." Rocky felt stupid defending such a wonderful person as Adrian to such a creep.

"Take 'er to the zoo. Retards like the zoo," the creep added irritatingly.

Rocky turned to Gazzo for help, "Does the bum have to say that?"

The bodyguard reddened. He could dish it out, but he couldn't take it. Gazzo motioned to the bodyguard to relax.

"Buddy's in a bad mood," Gazzo explained.

"He's always in a bad mood." Then laughing at Buddy's venomous expression, Rocky said, "Count ya' blessin's. Ya' a healthy person—ya' legs work, ya' hands work."

The expression on the bodyguard's face became more set; he stared at Rocky with murderous eyes. "I don't like ya' face!"

"Don't like yours neither," Rocky replied.

"Kiss my ass!"

"Move your shoulders down!" Rocky said.

Gazzo stepped out of the car followed by Rocky. "Buddy's got a thing against ya, Rock. Some people just hate for no reason, y'know. Here's fifty bucks— you an' the girl have a nice time."

"Thanks, Mr. Gazzo."

He entered his apartment and Gazzo drove off, tearing up the street.

Meanwhile, fate had slowed down and was trailing Rocky. There was a hell of a lot more than a fifty-dollar gratuity in it for him. Luckily, he was unaware of the shape of things to come, or he might not have spent an hour watching the turtles slide off the rock in their bowl; he might have been bursting out of his skin with anxiety and looking around for a newer, more expensive skin that could never be marred. (The right skin, on the right person, lasts a lifetime, no matter what happens.)

4

An amber day: mild, smooth, like twelve-year-old Scotch. Fine-grained, as the sunlight strained through polluted space, making all of Philadelphia look like an old sepia photo. Apollo Creed who was definitely sepia, but not old and not a photo—though his features were well known throughout the world—sat on the plush couch in Jergens' office, poring over a large record book.

"How 'bout this Billy Snow?" he asked.

"Fouls," Jergens replied.

"How 'bout this Big Chuck Smith?"

Mr. James, Apollo's trainer, who was sitting right beside Apollo, remarked in a weary voice, "Too old, dull fighter." Then pointing at a name, he suggested, "Bobby Judge is a good boy."

Apollo shook his head, "Um, no . . . I don't feel heat from that name: Judge, sludge, probably a drudge. Whut else we got?"

"Joe Czack was a good prospect," Jergens said hopefully.

"Still don't feel no heat," Apollo said again.

Discouraged, getting to the bottom of the list of possibilities, Jergens asked, "Exactly what are you looking for, Apollo?"

Apollo leaned forward. "This man." Then in an amused tone, "The Italian Stallion—he's my man."

"Rocky Balboa? His record's poor," Jergens interjected.

Apollo was not moved. "Don't matter. That name, 'the Italian Stallion'—it's right on." Then slapping his thigh in amusement at his own line of thought, Apollo asked, "Who discovered America? An Italian, right? So, man, what could be better than to get it on with one of his ancestors? Apollo Creed meets the Italian Stallion—sounds like a damn monster movie! Shit—I'll carry the bambino for three rounds, just dust him off a bit, then drop him like a bad habit."

Relieved, everyone in the room laughed. Jergens broke out a bottle of sour mash that, naturally, Apollo Creed did not share. He did not imbibe, he only ate kosher meat, and when he trained he went to sleep early every night and was up before dawn. He said that he owed a lot of his strength and ease of mind to proper sexual activities. He had never defined "proper," and definitely did not have to define sexual activities—beautiful women surrounded him at all times, and training camp was no exception.

The same November twenty-seventh, only it was dusk: It crept in on little feet, crawling back to mother night, who had already put on her house slippers and was pulling the curtains closed. Father night was probably tanking up at Andy's bar, where you couldn't tell night from day anyway, but he had a star in his pocket for the mortal Rocky, who couldn't find his way in the dark without it. There is a kind of poetry in bad poetry: dusk, night, stars—why not? That's part of life, isn't it?

Rocky and Paulie walked toward Paulie's house. Even though it was cold and dark, a group of kids were playing an energetic game of halfball (a variation of stickball).

Pretending to throw a ball, Rocky boasted, "I use ta be deadly at halfball."

Paulie grimaced, "I hate the friggin' game. I'd like ta be deadly at softball."

"What kinda business?" Rocky asked.

Paulie held out his hands; the joints were swollen, and the skin over them was inflamed. He tried to make a fist, but his thick hands could hardly bend. "Look at my hands. See 'em—inflamed joints. Walkin' in an' out of a freezer carryin' meat plays hell on the joints. It ain't even arthritis."

Sympathetically, Rocky said, "Maybe ya should see a doctor."

Paulie, angered that Rocky hadn't got the gist of what he meant, shouted, "I don't need a doctor, I need a different job! A job where I don't have to spend most of my time in a refrigerator like a slab of bloody meat."

"Yeah, maybe another job is the best thing," Rocky agreed.

"Do me a favor, talk to Gazzo. Tell him I'm a friend an' would do a good job. Tell him I ain't bothered by nothin' an' would be a great collector— bustin' bones don't bother me, unless they're my own. Tell him I'm a good worker," Paulie said.

Rocky didn't like the idea. Gazzo wouldn't listen

to him. "Gazzo's got to come to you," he answered cautiously.

"I'm askin' ya to go to him. As a favor." Paulie stopped walking for a moment and faced Rocky. Rocky turned away. He was getting uptight. Paulie had no right to force the issue.

"Gazzo's gotta come to you," he repeated dully; then, with a brighter outlook, "Hey Paulie, it's a bad job, you could get hurt, and it ain't steady, and people get to hate ya. Do what ya do now—and see a doctor."

They continued past the Atomic Hoagie Shop. The hoagie hadn't taken off yet. Its tail sparkled and burst according to a simple timing device. A group of young men were pitching quarters on the sidewalk outside. Rocky noticed Marie, the kid from the night before. She took a deep drag on her cigarette and faced in the opposite direction from Rocky. The gang smiled and continued to pitch quarters. Anger and disappointment registered across Rocky's face. Paulie noticed the expression and the way Rocky sort of stared at the young people.

"You know her?" he asked, indicating Marie.

Rocky shrugged, and the two men moved off. Only the sound of metal—quarter hitting quarter, or quarter hitting wall—filled the night air. One thing Rocky could never understand was why nobody could take good advice or accept help, why'd they rather go right straight down the drain—like Marie.

Paulie lived in an apartment at the top of a dimly lit four-story walkup. "Hey, ya ever run up and down the steps for exercise?" Rocky asked.

"I watch TV for exercise," Paulie replied, already out of breath.

"Ya' sistah know I'm comin'?" Rocky asked, hoping she wouldn't be too surprised.

"Yeah, sure. She's very excited." Somehow Paulie didn't sound too convincing.

He unlocked the apartment door, and they went in, Rocky hanging back, a bit stiff. Adrian stepped out of the kitchen, holding a large serving spoon. Her hair was loose and disheveled, her face flushed from being too close to the flame, and her apron was streaked with food. The TV was on, playing to no one. Adrian let it play because it kept her company, gave her the illusion that someone else was in the house. As long as the TV was there in full sight and sound, she was hardly ever lonely. Hardly ever.

Adrian eyed Rocky. She became visibly upset at his unexpected presence. Paulie had lied to Rocky. She hadn't known about his visit. "Paulie, you're late!" she said sharply. She looked at Rocky again. This wasn't the way she planned to see him out of the pet shop; she couldn't have looked more a mess.

"Did you call the hospital?" Paulie sassed. Then turning to Rocky uneasily, he said, "If I'm ten minutes late, she calls the hospital."

Adrian ran into the bedroom. Paulie followed her. It had been stupid and cruel of him to spring Rocky on her that way, trapping her in the unromantic, ordinary surroundings of their apartment. Rocky could hear them arguing. Over the argument he heard a sports broadcast. He increased the volume, and the commentator was saying, ". . . unfortunate luck for fifth-ranked heavyweight

Mac Lee Green. The slugging fighter acquired a serious fracture in his left hand after an aggressive day of sparring. Champion Apollo Creed says he'll be shopping for another victim to fill Green's vacancy for the Bicentennial Championship fight to be held in Philly next month. By the way, rumor has it that this will be the most widely viewed sporting event in the entire world—and that includes the Super Bowl, folks. Today the U.S. swimmers set a new . . ."

Meanwhile, the argument between brother and sister continued in the bedroom. Rocky couldn't help but overhear: The walls were paper thin and their voices carried easily.

"Paulie, why didn't you tell me you were bringing him home? Look at me, I'm not ready for this," Adrian shouted.

"Like it would make a difference if you were, right? This guy's a friend, and now he's takin' ya out." Paulie sounded like he was boss. The whole thing settled.

"No . . . I can't!" Adrian sobbed.

"Ya, ya' goin' outta this bedroom, an' I don't wanna know from nothin'." Paulie's voice was softer. Rocky imagined he was putting his arm around his sister's shoulders, giving her courage to come out. He wasn't. He was standing there biting his nails and thinking how he could jolt her into some kind of living.

"Paulie, please . . ."

"Hey," he whined, "I want ya out instamatically. I'm sicka lookin' at ya hangin' around like a friggin' spider. Go out. Live! Enjoy life!"

"Like you?"

"Don't get wise with me. I want ya to stop bein'

a loser." He began to shove her toward the door.

"I can't go out," she insisted.

"Why?" Paulie asked.

"Paulie, it's Thanksgiving. I've got a turkey in the oven."

In a fury, Paulie rushed out of the bedroom and entered the kitchen. Grabbing a large fork, he opened the oven door, speared the turkey, and heaved the dripping bird out the window. If ever a bird needed wings, that bird did. It dropped like a fragrant stone into the filthy back alley, landing on a pile of old mattresses, beer cans, vermin, and a dead cat. In a few minutes some cats had found their feast and were eating pot luck. Adrian was shattered. She locked the bedroom door and leaned against it, trembling. Gone was the chestnut stuffing she had filled the bird with, and gone was the drumstick she had coveted. All that was left was a greasy pan and a panting brother—and Rocky, whom she really wanted to go out with but was too embarrassed to acknowledge.

Paulie yelled, "Ya want the bird, go out in the alley an' eat the bird. I want ya outta the house. Enjoy ya' friggin' life. Ya hungry, Rock?"

"Maybe ya better forget it," Rocky mumbled.

"Forget nothin'. Here, talk to my sister, tell 'er somethin' nice."

Rocky walked over to Adrian's door and began to speak to her, "Yo, Adrian, it's me, Rocky. Ah, ah . . . ah, it's kinda hard for me to think of somethin' to say, y'know, 'cause I never talked to a door before. I mean, whatta ya say to a door?" He turned and began to walk off, "Maybe I better forget it."

"Try again, c'mon, try again," Paulie pleaded.

Rocky went to the door and began again, "Ah, Adrian, I know ya ain't too happy at this moment, but would ya do me a favor? I ain't got nobody to spend Thanksgivin' with. How 'bout you an' me goin' out? Get somethin' to eat, maybe laugh a little, who knows. Would ya like, I dunno, to go out together?"

When Adrian opened the door a few minutes later, she already had her coat on.

"We'll have a good time," Rocky reassured her.

Paulie opened the front door and ushered them out with an encouraging smile.

"What's ya' sister like to do?" Rocky asked Paulie secretly.

"Ice-skate," Paulie replied.

The rink was located on the top floor of an office building in the business district. An old lady seated at an organ was playing peppy ice-skating tunes.

"I love waltzes," Adrian said. "Hey, can ya help me lace these up?"

Rocky, who wasn't too good with his fingers, managed to lace the rented pair of skates well enough. Just being around Adrian's ankles got him hot. He decided to be casual. "Don't ya need to go to some special school to learn to work with so many animals?"

"I only went to high school," Adrian replied after a pause.

"How d'ya like workin' with the puppies?" Rocky had found an easy topic of conversation and would follow it through to the end.

"Fine," Adrian said.

"Say, how 'bout the snakes, you miss them, too?"

Adrian didn't respond; she was testing the skates

to see whether they were laced tight enough. Without a good fit, anyone could twist his ankle. The skates the rink rented out were not so terrific; they should have been replaced long ago. Adrian glided away from the rail, then back again to Rocky.

"You scared a snakes?" Rocky asked.

"Not really. Can I ask you a question?" Her face had taken on a serious mien.

"A question? Absolutely."

"Why do you fight?"

Rocky wasn't sure whether she just wanted to know or whether she was judging him. Lots of women couldn't stand the sport.

" 'Cause I can't sing or dance."

Adrian walked onto the ice with clumpy little steps. Rocky followed. He wasn't wearing skates; he had never been on ice in his life, and he had vowed he would still not be on ice when he died. He shuffled along in his street shoes, hoping no one would notice his clumsy imitation of ice-skating. "Where'd ya learn this?" Rocky asked. Adrian was almost as bad as he was.

"I've only done it once or twice."

"No kiddin'. Like I was sayin' before, fightin' use to be tops with me, but no more." Rocky hadn't been saying that before; he had been thinking it, until the thought got louder and louder and came out of his mouth. "All I wanted to prove was I wasn't no tomato—that I had the stuff to make a good pro."

"And you never got the chance?"

"I ain't cryin' . . . I still fight. Do it like a hobby." Some hobby, Rocky thought. He allowed himself to feel sorry for himself, but for only half a second. A shaking instructor, who wasn't the least bit fooled by Rocky's imitation of ice-skating in leather soled shoes, glided over, and made a grand sweeping slide in front of Rocky.

"If you want to remain on the ice, put on skates," he said in an overbearing way.

"Yeah, be off in a minute." Turning to Adrian he continued, "See, I'm a southpaw an' most pugs won't fight a southpaw . . . Southpaw means left-handed." They moved away from the instructor, who watched to see that Rocky was headed toward the railing. "Things probably worked out for the best, right?" He turned to Adrian for approval.

"But you never had a chance to prove yourself," she had guessed that he hadn't meant his last statement.

"Absolutely!" Rocky said, pressing her arm warmly. It was well shaped under the thin woolen weave of her sweater, a suggestion of muscle and firm young flesh, even though she too was thirty years old. Lifting animals had helped to keep her in shape.

Rocky removed a crumpled photo from his wallet, and proudly showed it to Adrian, "That's me fightin' Big Baby Crenshaw. I lost, but it's a nice picture, don't ya think?" Adrian did a slight turn. Rocky nearly fell. "I hit hard, real hard, but I'm a southpaw, an' nobody wants to fight a southpaw, so . . ."

The irate instructor sped over and purposely stopped in such a manner that ice sprayed the front of Rocky's pants.

"Either put on skates now, or get off the ice. Do it, or I'll have you ejected from the rink, fella!"

Rocky ignored him and slid off with Adrian. The instructor was outraged. Turning to Adrian, who

was about half an inch away, Rocky began to tell
her his life history, the only history he knew pretty
well without having to read up on it. "Y'know how
I got started in the fight racket?"

"By accident?" Adrian guessed.

"My ol' man, who was never the sharpest, told
me I weren't born with much brain, so I better use
my body."

For the first time Adrian laughed.

"What's funny?" Rocky demanded. He thought
what he said was kind of sad—imagine sayin' a
thing like that to a kid! Puts him in a paper bag
right away, and not everyone can fight their way
out of a paper bag.

"My mother told me just the opposite. She said,
'You weren't born with much of a body, so you'd
better develop your brain.' "

"Oh, yeah—maybe we had the same mother an'
father."

The couple passed close to the angry instructor.
Rocky saw that the man was about to hassle them
again, so just as the instructor was closing in, about
to speak, Rocky looked straight ahead but gave
the man a casual straight-arm. The instructor
landed on his butt. Adrian and Rocky glided off
. . . off into the night trolley . . . onto the shiny old
wicker seats with tickly horsehair escaping through
the broken straw . . . into the romantic intimacy of
sitting side by side in an empty vehicle, reading the
advertisements above the seats opposite them and
pressing thighs, hearing the steel tracks shudder
and the trolley keep its shaky course down South
Street . . . into the warm wonder of saying things
to each other they had never said to anyone else
. . . in the trolley.

"Some people are very shy by nature," Rocky stated.

"I suppose."

"I would say you're very shy by nature," he patted her hand.

"I suppose."

"Some people think bein' shy is a disease, but it don't bother me." He hoped his approval would bring her out.

"It doesn't bother me either," she agreed.

"Then why did I bother bringing it up? 'Cause I'm dumb, that's why. Y'know, I think we make a real sharp coupla coconuts. I'm dumb and you're shy."

"It's just as hard for me to understand why anybody wants to be a fighter."

"Ya gotta be a little soft to wanna be a pug. It's a racket where ya' almost guaranteed to end up a bum," Rocky said.

"I don't think you're a bum," Adrian said sweetly.

"I'm at least half a bum. Yeah, fightin' is a crazy racket. The roughest part is the mornin' after." Rocky shivered involuntarily at the memory of many mornings after.

"Morning after?"

"After a rough fight, ya' nothin' but a large wound. Sometimes I feel like callin' a taxi to drive me from my bed to the bathroom. Ya' eyes hurt, ya' ears hurt, ya' hair even hurts. But the thing I'm proud of is I been in over sixty fights an' never had a busted nose. Bent and twisted an' bitten, but never broke. That's rare."

"Why do you do it if it hurts so bad?"

"Guess," Rocky said.

After a pause, during which all sorts of answers came to Adrian's mind, she said, " 'Cause you can't sing or dance?"

"Would ya care for a glass of water?" Rocky went to the fridge, where he kept a bottle of water cold.

"No thanks." Adrian looked around for the first time and saw the mirror above Rocky's dresser. She saw a very young photo of Rocky stuck into the mirror frame. He was handsome and smooth-faced, wearing a shirt and tie, proud of himself. Rocky stepped up behind Adrian. His face reflected in the mirror. "That's the Italian Stallion when he was a baby."

Rocky put on his cheap record player, danced over to the turtle bowl, and reached in. "Here's the guys I was tellin' you about. This is Cuff an' Link." Both turtles were cupped in one palm.

"I was the one sold them to you," Adrian said.

Very embarrassed, Rocky went into a song and dance of recall. "Oh, yeah, I bought the whole kit. Yeah, ya sold me the turtles, the bowl, an' the mountain. I had to get rid of the mountain 'cause the turtles kept falling off."

"Do you have a phone?" Adrian interrupted.

"I had it pulled. People callin' all the time. Who needs it. Who'd ya wanna call?"

"I wanna let my brother know where I am." She was getting edgy, wanted to touch home.

"Do ya really wanna call?" Rocky asked, annoyed.

"Yes, I do."

"You sure?"

"Yes."

"Why?"

"I think Paulie might be worried."

"I'll call your brother," Rocky offered. He flung open the window, and bellowing like a foghorn, called, "Yo! Paulie, ya' sister's with me! I'll call ya later." He closed the window and faced Adrian. She was not smiling. His clumsy attempt at humor had only frightened her. "What's the matter? Don't ya like the place?" Rocky gently joked.

"The apartment's fine," Adrian remonstrated.

"It's only temporary," Rocky continued.

"It's not that, Rocky." She looked forlorn.

"What's the problem? You don't like me? Don't like the turtles? What is it?"

"I don't think I belong here."

"It's okay."

"No, I don't belong here."

"It's all right. You're my guest."

"I've never been in a man's apartment before," Adrian admitted.

"They're all the same," he declared.

"I'm not sure I know you well enough . . . I don't think I'm comfortable."

"Yo, I ain't comfortable either," Rocky admitted. "But I'm willin' to make the best of an uncomfortable situation."

"I should leave." She began to walk toward the door.

Stopping her, Rocky whispered into her ear, "How would ya feel if I asked ya to take off your glasses."

Dumbstruck, Adrian exclaimed, "What?"

"The glasses . . . please." She let him remove her glasses and looking deeply into her eyes, he said, "You got nice eyes."

"They're small."

"Small, but a good color."

"Thank you," Adrian mumbled.

"Do me another favor? Could ya let the hair down?"

"Why are you doing this?" Adrian asked, as she let her long, deep-brown hair fall.

"Ah, that's nice," he whispered, "a movie star."

"Don't tease me," Adrian pleaded. A sob escaped her. She wanted so much to be pretty and admired. Rocky put his arms around her, like a magic fence.

"I wanna kiss ya. Ya don't have to kiss me back if ya don't feel like it," Rocky whispered.

5

So Rocky had a lady. He felt different. Someone cared. The day was welcome; and he strolled down the street like a king who had just increased his territory. His walk was jaunty, his coat buttoned with all the buttons in the right buttonholes, and his eyes glowed with happiness. He was on his way to Goldmill's Gym; hadn't even given his usurped locker a thought. Out front a group of young blacks stopped rapping and studied Rocky as he passed. Rocky wondered why. They'd never paid him any attention before. He skipped up the steps and entered the gym. In a matter of seconds he was noticed, and the other athletes stared at him in wonderment. Rocky thought that maybe his new-found happiness was so obvious that everyone was drawn to it like a magnet. The big black heavy-weight contender, Dipper, had a weird reaction: He threw his towel down in disgust and turned away. Mike quickly approached Rocky.

"Hey, Rock, what happened?"

"Happened? 'Bout what?" Rocky responded. He was confused.

Mickey Goldmill stepped out of his office and inquired, "Did ya get the message, kid?"

"Message? What message?" The mystery was deepening.

Mickey pulled a card from his breast pocket and handed it to Rocky. "A rep from Miles Jergens Promotions was lookin' for ya. They need sparrin' partners for Creed."

"Ya puttin' me on?" Rocky was incredulous. Just to be in close promixity to the champ would be—well, like a dream come true. Sometimes greatness rubs off on you.

"Here's the card," Mickey offered the proof.

"When was they here?"

" 'Bout an hour ago."

"Probably lookin' for sparin' partners," Rocky repeated dumbly.

"I said that before," Mickey said, irritated at Rocky.

Rocky turned away and jogged out of the gym. He could feel his blood circulating, his muscles trembling, his chest expanding. A fine sweat soaked through his shirt as he ran. This time he was running toward something, not away—he was running toward the glorious future he had once promised himself.

Mickey, pessimistic as usual (and he had lots of reason to be that way), fumbled with his rosary beads like an old woman. "Waste of life," he mumbled as each hard, round, pierced-glass bead passed through his fingers. Penance put him at ease. Between his own thoughts he threw in a few Hail Marys.

Rocky stepped off a bus in midtown. He hurried down Broad Street. Every few steps he broke into a trot. People passed by him in one blurry rush. Finally he came to the skyscraper that had been scraping the sky for forty-five years, its Art Deco tower gliding downward from a sharp point to pseudo-Egyptian geometric ornamentation. The hall of the office building was ordinary enough: a candy-stand near the elevators, a flat directory behind glass, and an elevator captain in an elevator captain uniform watching the elevator bank of colored lights as they climbed up and down a master control board.

"Jergens Promotions?" Rocky asked.

"Tenth floor," the man replied, deftly touching his cap's visor.

In a few seconds, Rocky burst into the office of Miles Jergens Promotions, a wild look in his eyes. The secretary was slightly startled by Rocky's excited expression.

"May I help you?" she asked, watching him carefully. If he turned out to be a nut, she could press the tiny emergency button beside her desk, and security would come running to help.

Rocky handed her the business card he had picked up at the gym.

"Your name, please?" The secretary continued, all business.

"Balboa, Rocky Balboa."

Rising slowly and smoothing, her stretch jersey skirt over an already smoothly stretched body, she went into Jergens' office. Rocky let his eyes wander over a multitude of sports pictures that were hanging on all four walls. When the secretary returned, she told him he could go in. Rocky thanked her, straightened his jacket, ran a comb through his hair, and went for the office.

"Hello, Mr. Balboa. I'm Miles Jergens. Please have a seat." Mr. Jergens put as much warmth into his greeting as he could muster. Warmth wasn't his strong point.

"Mr. Balboa . . ."

"Rocky," Rocky interjected.

"Rocky, do you have any representation? A manager?"

"No, just me."

"Rocky, would you be interested in . . ." Jergens began, and Rocky interrupted again in his eagerness to seem on top of things.

"Sparrin'?" he said swiftly.

"Excuse me?" Jergens didn't know what Rocky meant.

"I know ya need sparrin' partners. I'm very available."

"I'm sure you are," Jergens agreed.

"Absolutely. Sparrin' with the champ would be an honor. Y'know what?" Rocky wanted to sell himself bad. He couldn't believe that he was already chosen. Maybe the bad fairy would come and drag him out of Jergens' office. Maybe it was some kind of joke.

"What?" Jergens asked.

"I wouldn't take no cheap shots. I'd be a good sparrin' partner," Rocky said proudly.

Jergens was amused. He lit a cigar, and wetting the brown leaf wrapper, sucked on his fat, tobacco pacifier. "Rocky," he said from behind the fragrant smokescreen rising from his cigar, "Rocky, would you be interested in fighting Apollo Creed for the championship?"

Rocky wasn't sure he had heard what he heard. So he pretended he hadn't heard it. "Like I said, I'd make a boss sparrin' mate."

"Did you hear what I said?" Jergens asked.

"Sure, an' I'm smart enough to know that no sparrin' partner should take cheap shots at the champ. He's just there to help condition the man."

Jergens wondered whether he had made a mistake choosing Rocky; maybe the guy was wacky. "Not spar," he enunciated carefully. "I'm asking whether you would be interested in fighting Creed for the championship."

The weight of the statement came crashing down on Rocky. For one long moment he became a basket case as he pondered the statement. Then, regaining some of his senses, he replied, "Ah . . . I ah . . . sure, absolutely."

Jergens leaned across the desk and offered Rocky his hand. The biggest deal in Rocky's life was about to be consummated.

Rocky, Adrian, and Paulie met at Paulie's apartment for an evening of entertainment in front of the boob tube. Its flickering light and madly circumscribed activities held their attention hypnotically. Apollo Creed was being interviewed. It wasn't as if Rocky didn't know what Creed was going to say—after all, he was in the interview, too—but it gave him a thrill to pretend it was news to him.

"How do you like the City of Brotherly Love?" a reporter asked Creed.

"I like my Philadelphia brothers. An' I'm patriotic!" Creed had to duck to the left to avoid a thrusting microphone. Then he continued, in mock seriousness, "If yo don't back up I'm gonna send yo home with a microphone in yo' nose!"

The reporter laughed but kept the mike right up front, near Apollo's mouth. "Why did you agree to fight a man who has virtually no chance of winning?" he asked.

Apollo stuck one hand inside his jacket, like a bigger, tougher, darker Napoleon. "If history proves one thing, everybody gotta chance. Didn't yo' all ever hear of David an' Goliath? 'Course, I woulda knocked out Goliath. I wouldn't a needed no slingshot. Mah fists are made of stone . . . they can do the job alone!" He began throwing his fists into the air as if they were stones. It was easy to imagine them making a thick parabola in the sky and then landing with a cruel thud on Goliath's head.

"Is it just a coincidence that you're fighting a white man on the first celebrated day of the country's bicentennial?" the reporter insinuated.

Not wanting to start a political fracas, Apollo answered, "The same coincidence that he's fightin' a black man."

"Then what are your feelings about the challenger?"

"He's Italian." Apollo looked very serious, mock serious.

"What does that mean?" The reporter wondered.

"It means, if he can't fight, I bet he can cook!"

In front of the TV Rocky and Adrian laughed. It was Paulie who took offense. "Do me a favor. His lungs—punch 'em out."

Rocky's interview filled the screen. He looked nervous under the hot lights. There were beads of sweat on his forehead; no one had put makeup on him or styled his hair the way they do with politicians, so he didn't look embalmed or theatrically tan. He looked naturally funky and foul.

"This is your largest payday ever. How do you feel about it?" the reporter asked.

"Feel? I dunno . . . happy." He smiled to show how happy he was. The smile got stuck and became more of a grimace.

"How will you fight Apollo Creed?" persisted the reporter.

Rocky, his mind elsewhere, answered, "Creed's great, ain't he? I'll do what I can."

"And where did you get the name 'Italian Stallion'?"

"Get it? I thought of it 'bout eight years ago, when I was eatin' dinner."

"Is it true the most you've ever made in a prizefight is five hundred dollars?"

"Four hundred," Rocky corrected, as if there were someone out there watching who would punish him if he allowed the lie to stand. "But that was a long time ago," he added.

"And now your payday will be one hundred and fifty thousand dollars. Any comment?"

True to form, Rocky didn't react the way the reporter had set the question up. He didn't want to say he was the luckiest guy in the world, or thank God, or anything. "Listen, I wanna say hi to my girlfriend . . . Yo, Adrian!"

Adrian blushed and laughed, "Oh, Rocky!"

Paulie was embarrassed for Rocky. "Christ!" He shook his head.

"You didn't," Adrian said, pleased. Her private association with the contender was now public, making her a kind of celebrity, too.

"Sure I did—you heard," Rocky said, nudging her affectionately. "I want the whole world to know!"

They continued to watch the remainder of the interview. The head commentator, Steward Neham, a college moron, a silver-haired jock who was thirty years past his false prime, looked directly into the camera, his voice pompous, his enunciation boringly crisp and clear—a thoroughly boring professional. Steward was not worth the $400,000 the station paid him to be a news personality; he was a sadistic closet-case who took great pleasure in belittling others who were better than this turd could ever hope to be. Even his tailor did not respect him, and spent hours making suits that would hide Steward's milky fat. As he spoke his capped teeth flashed forth: "Another cheap show report, a bicentennial fight . . . January first. It will be the first sporting event on our two hundreth birthday and is already being called by many the greatest farce in sports history. If this poor bum lasts more than a minute I would say he's on borrowed time. It's matches like this, with their exorbitant prices, that give sports a bad name. Not only is this match bad, people, it's sad! . . . What's a Rocky Balboa? And is there a cure? At the State Athletic Commission, Steward Neham reporting."

Irately, Paulie said, "The guys's a friggin' moron."

"Why?" asked Rocky.

"Don't it matter none that faggot's makin' ya out a fool? I'd break that faggot's lips."

"It don't matter."

"He's takin' cheap shots!" Paulie said.

Again Rocky said, "It don't bother me none."

Another idea entered Paulie's head, something more practical than pride, a possible job for himself. He thought he'd hit on his friend for assistance: "Yo, Rock, now ya'll be lookin' for people to help, right?"

"Help what?"

"Y'know, to help keep ya livin' clean." He shut the TV off and stood in front of it, facing Rocky.

"I'll be okay," Rocky responded.

Paulie wouldn't let him go. "Ya gotta have a guy help ya exercise, mebbe somebody to be standin' by with a towel or run errands, y'know."

Self-pity filled Rocky and led him to a pretty stupid conclusion. "Hey, who cared about me yesterday, huh? I think I'm gonna train myself."

"Ain't never been done, Rock. Without havin' good people around, ya won't have such a good chance," Paulie explained.

Adrian didn't like her brother's pushy attitude; she felt that he was trying to discourage Rocky and take him for some easy bread. "Einstein flunked out of school—twice!"

"That so," Paulie said angrily.

Adrian continued with her list of geniuses who had fought against tremendous odds and won: "Roosevelt finished last in his class. Beethoven was deaf, an' Helen Keller was deaf, dumb, and blind. I think Rocky has a chance—a good chance!"

As Rocky stood in the doorway, he kissed Adrian good night.

As he moved down the stairway, and thought of milky fat Steward Neham, his voice bounced up the stairs with the resonance of empty beer cans: "How'd ya like hearin' ya' name on TV?"

"I don't know. I was shocked. Why did you do that?"

"Ya puttin' me on, right?"

"Absolutely," Adrian called, smiling to herself. "What time should I expect you?"

" 'Bout seven."

"I'll be waiting." Adrian leaned over the balustrade to try to catch a glimpse of Rocky on the ground floor.

Rocky yelled up to Adrian, "Y'know how I said that stuff on television didn't bother me?"

"Yes," Adrian replied.

"It did," Rocky admitted. As he finished, he again thought about Steward Neham. Damn pansy. Cheapshot artist. He left the building and slammed the door. His anger resounded throughout the apartment house, then dissipated.

Outside the Atomic Hoagie Shop, Rocky, Gazzo and the bodyguard stood eating hot, fat sandwiches. Between bites, Rocky said, "Y'know I won't be able to work for ya no more."

"Hey, if a good man can make a better life, let him make it." Gazzo hadn't known many like that; most of the people he dealt with went from bad to worse. Rocky had never caused him any grief; he really wished him well.

"I feel bad about walkin'." The thinly sliced onions were slipping out of the sides of his submarine roll, so he had to trim the sides of his sandwich by biting the fallout with his teeth; it looked as if he were playing the harmonica.

"Take your shot, kid. You got money for trainin' expenses?" Gazzo asked.

"A few bucks," Rocky answered.

Gazzo took out a wad and peeled off several bills. One might have thought he were removing wilted leaves from a cabbage, so casual did he seem to be.

"Here's five hundred—put it in your glove," he said.

"Do I have to pay juice?" Rocky asked.

Gazzo looked at his bodyguard as if to imply, "Why's this guy asking such a foolish question?" Then he and his human arsenal stepped into his white Caddy. Gazzo, seeing Rocky still there at the curb, leaned out of the car window and, smiling, said, "Does Santa Claus charge juice? Merry Christmas. Now, how's about my present—ya gonna win?"

"Gonna try," Rocky promised.

"Listen, kid, I'm with ya, ya know, I'm with ya . . . Italian, we're blood. You kill this rug. We Guineas gotta show these Afro-Americans where it's at. Give it your best shot 'cause I want ya to prove it to these bums on the corner that my man can't be beat by this rug. Ya got any action on the side?" Gazzo asked.

"No action," Rocky replied.

"Ya gettin' one hundred and fifty grand, killer. Ya got any plans for it? Whatta ya think? Ya like to put it on the street, make it work for ya?" Gazzo had leaned back in the car, and Rocky practically had to get on his knees and lean into the window to see and talk to him.

"I'm gonna do somethin' with it," Rocky said.

"Sure, you do what ya want. Stay away from the stock market." Gazzo laughed.

"Black market?" Rocky asked mistakenly.

"Same thing. Ya know, Rock, remember when we was kids we fought together. An' I wasn't well an' ya had to beat up that Irish kid—what's his name?—Gallager. I bought a suit and became a businessman. You put on gloves. An' I remember your mama almost cried, may she rest in peace. An' your ol' man, who said ya had no brains. I'd like to lay my hands on that bastard. You ain't never had any luck. Even when I owned you in '66 you never had luck. But now I think you might be gettin' some luck, kid. Whatta ya think?"

Rocky smiled and said, "Yo, gonna show, Tony?"

"Where else am I gonna go?" Then turning to his bodyguard, Gazzo ordered, "Bet three grand on Rocky."

Finally the bodyguard said something. "He's a bum—are you kiddin'?" It was the wrong thing to say. Gazzo slapped him hard across the cheek.

"No, I'm not kiddin'!" he said.

At home, Rocky did what he had done for a long time, his lonely routine: flipped on his record player, fed his turtles—"Hey, look who's home!" But there was something different: Rocky noticed two telegrams laying inside the threshold. He approached them with a sense of awe. The envelopes were as starched and clean as a yellow organdy dress. Rocky tried to peek into the lozenge-shaped windows to read the telegrams before he had ripped the envelopes open. Settling on the bed, he opened them. They were strangers, congratulating him on his good fortune. Suddenly he felt chilly, as if a wind were blowing through his bones; it hit him that his life was now public, and anybody who wanted to could find him, or write to him, even follow him. He didn't like the exposure. When someone knocked at his door at that moment, he recoiled, then opened it. Surprise of surprises—Mickey Goldmill, the gym owner stood framed in the doorway. "I seen the light. I figured somebody was home," he said stiffly.

To Rocky, Mickey Goldmill was a luminary, and his arrival nonplused him. "Hey, Mickey, whatta ya doin' here? Here, sit down." He tossed some soiled clothing from a mangled armchair and ushered Mr. Goldmill to it. "Best seat in the house. Hey, Mick, this is too much."

"How do ya mean?" Mickey asked.

"I'm use to seein' ya at the gym, but seein' ya here, in my house, it's kinda outta joint."

It embarrassed Rocky to have an outsider see how he lived; except for the fact that he had a roof and four walls, he might have been one of those rag pickers who lived out of paper bags and slept in doorways. But on watching Goldmill, he guessed that the old man had something important on his mind.

"Listen, Rocky, you're a very lucky guy," Mickey said.

"Yeah."

"What's happened is freak luck," Goldmill continued.

"Freak luck for sure," acknowledged Rocky. He

began pacing the room, wondering what Goldmill wanted.

"Look at all them other fighters. Real good boys. Good records. Colorful. Fight their hearts out for peanuts. But who cared? Nobody. They got it shoved in their back door. Nobody ever gives them a shot at the title."

Uneasily, Rocky said, "Freak luck is a strange thing."

Mickey, instead of talking with Rocky about what to do when freak luck strikes, found his attention drawn to the turtles. "Whatta those?"

"Turtles—domestic turtles."

"Turtles? You ever had turtle soup?" Mickey asked.

"Things ain"t never been that bad," Rocky said dryly. He enjoyed kidding Mickey.

"Rock, I'm here tellin' ya to be very smart with this shot. Like the Bible says, ya don't get no second chance." He looked hard into Rocky's eyes and continued. "Ya need a manager. An adviser. I been in the racket fifty years. I done it all; there ain't nothin' about the world of pugilism that ain't livin' up here." Mickey, lit a half-smoked cigar. The smell of it obliterated any other odor that may have existed in the room. Mickey seemed to breath more deeply when he inhaled the smoke; air only made him cough.

At a loss, and not wanting to hurt the old man, Rocky said, "Fifty years, huh?"

Mickey picked it up. "Fifty years. The rep is known around Philly, an' a good rep can't be bought, but I don't have to tell you that."

To change the subject, Rocky suggested, "How 'bout a glass of water?"

Mickey ignored him. "Rocky, d'ya know what I done?"

"What?"

Driving each word hard, Mickey recited his credits: "*I done it all.* I done an' seen everythin'. Believe what I'm tellin' ya. Ya shoulda seen the night in Brooklyn I smashed 'Ginny' Russo outta the ring, September 14, 1923—same night Firpo knocked Dempsey outta the ring. But who got the press? He did. He had a manager. September 14, 1923."

Softly, Rocky murmured, "Ya got a good mind for dates . . ."

But he didn't get a chance to continue: Mickey kept talking as in a dream, becoming more engrossed every minute, reliving the past. "Look at this face—twenty-one stitches over the left eye, thirty-four over the right. My nose was busted seventeen times, the last being the Sailor Mike fight New Year's Eve, 1940, in Camden, New Jersey. What a professional pastin' I give him. Here, read about it." He showed Rocky a tiny press clipping, then, pointing to his cauliflower ear, added, "An' he give me the vegetable on the ear. I got pain an' experience. An' you got heart—kinda remind me of Marciano, ya do."

Touched by this comparison, Rocky pointed to his most prized possession, the photo of Marciano. "Nobody ever said that. There's his picture."

Mickey, pressing his advantage, continued with the flattering comparison. "Yeah, ya kinda remind me of the Rock. Ya move like him." He had Rocky now, right smack in the middle of his fantasy. Nothing could have pleased Rocky more than what Mickey was saying.

"Really think so?" Rocky asked.

"Ya got heart," Mickey emphasized.

"Heart, but I ain't got no locker." He tried to embarrass Mickey. Mickey never would have taken Marciano's locker away. Rocky crouched, with his back against the wall—it made him look like a fallen gargoyle. Mickey either reserved his answer concerning Rockey's locker, or was too much into his monologue to stop and explain. He hadn't yet finished with the true and wonderful story of the career of Mickey Goldmill.

"Christ, I know this business, Rocky, when I was fightin' it was the dirtiest racket goin', see. Pugs like me was treated like fightin' dogs—throw ya in the pit an' for ten bucks ya try to kill each other. We had no management—fought in boxcars, in whorehouse basements, any joint with a floor. October 1931 I fought a bum who put a tack in the thumb of his glove an' punched so many holes in my face I had spit shootin' outta my cheeks. I never had no manager watchin' out for me. See that picture outside the gym? 'Mighty Mick,' that's me in my prime. I had all the tools. I coulda starched any lightweight husky on the East Coast. But I had no management. Nobody ever got to know how slick I was, but I had a head for business an' stashed a few bucks an' opened the gym. It's a dirt hole, I know it, but that an' a lotta scars is what I got to show for fifty years in the business, kid. Now you come along with this shot, an' I feel like it's me gettin' the shot I never got. An' now I got all this knowledge, I wanna give it ta ya so I can protect ya!"

The intensity of the old man made Rocky hot. Suddenly he felt as if he were wearing too much;

his underwear began to itch, and he couldn't get enough air into his lungs. He opened the window and stood there, just breathing.

Mickey continued, "Respect, I always dished ya respect."

"Ya give Dipper my locker," accused Rocky.

Almost begging, Mickey asked forgiveness. "I'm sorry, I . . . I made a mistake. Kid, I'm askin' man to man. I wanna be ya' manager."

Without looking at Mickey, Rocky answered coldly, "The fight's set. I don't need a manager."

Mickey's voice quavered with emotion as he pleaded his case. "Look, ya can't buy what I know. Ya can't. I've seen it all! I got pain and I got experience."

"I got pain and experience, too," Rocky said.

"Please, kid!"

"Whatever I got, I always got on the slide. This shot's no different. I didn't earn nothin', I got it on the slide. I needed your help about ten years ago when I was startin', but ya never helped me none." He wished the old man would blow away, far away where he couldn't ask him any favors.

Nervously handling the ashtray, Mickey dropped it. He kneeled to retrieve it and wearily remained on one knee, as if about to propose to an unyielding lover. "If ya was wantin' my help, why didn't ya ask? Just ask."

"I asked, but ya never heard nothin'!"

Mickey yelled, "Rocky, I'm seventy-six years old. Maybe you can be the winner I never was—your shot is my last shot!"

That got to Rocky. Holding back his emotion, he went into the bathroom and closed the door.

Mickey struggled to his feet and, like a beaten man, left. Several moments later Rocky came out of the bathroom and lowered himself into bed, feeling guilty as hell. He couldn't rest; the image of the old man down on his knees to him, Rocky, former bum whose luck had changed, ate away at him. He sprang up a second later, ran outside and up the block toward the shadowy and hunched figure of Mickey. When he caught up with him under the eerie yellow-green lamplight, Rocky placed an arm around Mickey's shoulders. It was better than a handshake, and it sealed the deal. Rocky would benefit from the old man's know-how, and the old man would get a new lease on life through Rocky. The Bible didn't say it, but Rocky thought it: "Let bygones be bygones." That was the way it was going to be.

6

AT EXACTLY FOUR o'clock the following morning, Rocky's alarm clock went off, shaking him out of a deep sleep. Not accustomed to rising so early, he staggered to his feet and made his way to the bathroom. Turning on the light, he gave the roaches quite a scare, and they scattered, rushing behind pipes and into the medicine cabinet. Some of them had already climbed behind the telegrams that Rocky had placed at the top of the mirror. Half-awake, Rocky filled the basin with icy water and submerged his face in it. Then he swayed to the fridge, removed a dozen eggs, and taking five of them in turn, cracked them into a bowl. His body quivered as he downed the raw eggs in one swill.

For his morning run, Rocky was dressed in a well-worn sweat suit with a hood, and gloves and sneakers. It was pitch black outside, and his steaming breath made puffy clouds that floated above him, then disappeared into the cold air. His form also appeared and disappeared as he ran down the street. He could be clearly seen only as he passed beneath the street lamps. Two garbage-men stopped hoisting cans to watch him pass—he was more interesting than the usual cats stalking fallen scraps of garbage.

The art museum stood at the top of a steep flight of stairs like a pyramid that has lost its point; anyway, it had nearly disappeared into the morning gray, and it wasn't Shangri-la. Rocky was not going to run up the steps to reach eternal youth, or any of that jazz; he just had to run up and down the steps to increase his stamina, strengthen his legs—legs that would ostensibly carry his battered and battering body around the ring. Being a contender, you can't just lay back and dream; Rocky knew that, so taking a deep breath, he started up. He started, but halfway up his legs gave way. So he brushed himself off and went down again. He was not discouraged; getting into shape is a gradual business; you keep at it, and one day you can do more than you thought possible.

At City Hall, Rocky veered to the river, pausing to heave great gusts of exhausted breaths. He threw several lazy jabs in the air and walked a while with his hands on his aching sides. Then he forced himself to run again. The day was a long time dawning, and it was still a dirty gray as Rocky headed along Spring Garden Street. He passed under an elevated train station, and the hurried, roaring, metallic grumble of the train passing overhead seemed to blend perfectly with his muscular running style.

The sky began to lighten as Rocky ran along

the piers and past anchored freighters; a giant
water rat hurried away as Rocky bore down on
him; the rat's legs were okay, he had four of them
to get him where he was going. If Rocky had had
four legs, he would have stayed in one place like a
chair and let Apollo Creed sit on him—you can't
get hurt that way. But he had two. . . .

At five-thirty, Rocky approached the loading
platform of the Eastern Packing Company. Alongside it were several boxcars. Rocky mounted the
ramp and knocked on the metal door. It soon
opened, and Paulie guided him inside. Paulie was
already drunk.

Inside the shipping office, Paulie asked, "How
ya feelin?"

"Tight," panted Rocky.

Paulie held up a bottle of whiskey. "Wanna
drink?"

"No," Rocky said without hesitation.

As two Puerto Rican employees of the Eastern
Packing Company entered, Paulie proudly pointed
Rocky out. "This is the guy who's fightin' Apollo
Creed."

"Good luck. Kill him, man!" Jose, one of the
men, said.

Drunkenly, like a cheerleader trying to remember the good old days but failing, Paulie
yelled, "Hip hip hooray! C'mon . . . Hip hip . . ."

"Hooray, man," Jose said, finishing the cheer
and walking away.

"Rock'll be comin' by every mornin' to pick
up some prime—can't train on that store crap."

Rocky smiled, and Paulie led him out of the
office and to the large metal door of a walk-in
refrigerator. They entered into a winter wonder-

land of heavy sides of beef, flayed and frozen, hanging from hooks that extended into darkness at the far end of the refrigerator. An overhead blower kept the place freezing cold.

The freezer did not so much resemble a modern torture chamber as a ballet captured at the moment of ascent, in ice: The racks could be slowly turned, causing the meat to sway thickly back and forth. A layer of fat covered each carcass, which was in turn covered with tiny ice crystals. This is what gave the refrigerator a festive air; this is what kept death fresh. An overhead blower caused the men to speak loudly, and caused the temperature to remain steady.

"If ya don't pay Gazzo, ya end up hangin' on the hook, right?" Paulie teased.

"Gazzo's a good man," Rocky insisted.

"Yeah? Then how 'bout you talk to 'im 'bout me?"

"Talk?"

"Please do me that favor!" Paulie begged.

Rocky, ignoring the urgency in Paulie's voice, casually answered, "Keep this job, ya eat better."

Paulie opened a jackknife and idly jabbed the hanging meat. He swilled some whiskey from the pint bottle he carried with him. He was working up a sly piece of conversation to coerce Rocky with: "Y'know, d'ya think you an' my sister . . . ah, doin' good together?"

"Whatta you think?" Rocky answered, uncomfortable and cooling off too fast. He could have used a muffler in there.

"Ain't sure. What's the story?" Paulie kept on.

"What?" Rocky asked.

"The story—what's happenin'?" Paulie sounded

like a man who had mulled it over for quite a while. "Ya really like her?"

"Sure I like her."

Laughing nervously, Paulie asked, "What's the attraction? I don't see it."

"I dunno. She fills gaps," Rocky said reflectively.

"What gaps?"

"She got gaps. I got gaps. Together we fill the gaps." Rocky felt that he was revealing too much; after all, it wasn't any of Paulie's business.

Suddenly, Paulie asked what he shouldn't have. "You ballin' her?"

Holding back a rush of anger, Rocky turned toward Paulie and hissed, "Don't talk dirty 'bout ya' sister!"

Tersely, knowing he was in dangerous territory, Paulie put it another way. "C'mon, ya screwin' her?"

From across the room Rocky looked him hard in the eye. "That's why I can't put ya together with Gazzo, 'cause ya talk too much, big mouth."

Paulie reddened. He stepped forward and slammed his fists into a slab of hanging beef. The beef moved back and forth no more than two inches in each direction, sluggishly denying it had been hit at all. The punching of the beef was a muted challenge to Rocky, and he responded by slamming his fists into the brittle ribs of the side of beef. This time the grotesque object swung in a wide arc like a hanging corpse, which it was, minus head and dead eyes staring blindly. Rocky moved along the line of corpses, hooking great punches that only he felt across his knuckles and up the entire length of his arm. His face revealed a concentration never seen before, as though he were locked in total battle.

"Hit the rump. The rump! Ya'll break the ribs!" Paulie hollered.

Rocky continued pounding, faster and faster, reaching the second row of beef; his fists acted as human meat tenderizers and made him grimace with every punch. As he moved into the dark recesses of the refrigerator, only the dull sounds of his pounding fists could be heard. It was as if he were destroying a malignant and hidden fear that appeared only to him. His fury could hardly be explained logically. As he worked his way to Paulie again, a sadistic Balanchine of bull-bodies, his choreography made every hanging beef swing, looking surrealistically alive.

"We do that to Creed an' they'll take us to jail for murder," Paulie shouted.

Rocky looked at his hands. They were drenched in blood—up to his elbows in blood—his own and the bull's. Paulie handed him a package of beef.

"Don't talk dirty 'bout ya' sister." Rocky took the package and ran out. Paulie looked after him with some fear, a lot of respect, and just the tiniest bit of resentment.

At the gym, Rocky, without his frozen carcasses of meat to pound, reverted to the old standby, the heavy bag. The noise in the gym was deafening since the gym was filled to capacity. Mickey stepped forward and removed a string from his pocket: "Stop! Stop! I can't stand it! It's clumsy. You're off balance." He motioned to Mike, handed him the string, and said, "Tie it to both ankles. Leave two feet of slack."

"I never had good footwork," Rocky said, apologizing to Mickey, as if Mickey hadn't noticed it before.

"Forget the footwork. You're off balance. The legs are sticking everywhere. Marciano had the same problem, an' the string cured it. When you can hit and move without breakin' the string, you'll have balance!" Mickey said. He didn't want to hear what Rocky never had, he wanted to see what Rocky did have.

"You'll be a very dangerous person," Mike added, and finished with the string.

Two young boys in street clothes interrupted Mickey. "Rocky could we have your autograph?" one asked.

"Sure," Rocky answered, pleased.

Mickey was not as pleased as Rocky; in fact he was irate. "Don't you boys ever interrupt when I'm conductin' business, or I'll kill you both. Go away." As suddenly as they had appeared, the boys disappeared—that was Mickey's magic. Turning to Rocky, who was still glowing with his new-found celebrity, Mickey shouted, "Autographs! Ya wanna be a writer or a fighter? Let's work."

"We got visitors," Mike cautioned.

Mickey strained his eyes to see Steward Neham and news cameramen entering his gym. Approaching them, he said, "Can I help you guys?"

The smug newscaster first turned to his cameramen; "Set the camera up over there." Then he said to Mickey, "I'm Steward Neham, which I'm sure you knew, and I'm covering the prefight training."

"I own the place," Mickey informed him.

Steward turned from Mickey and nodded to his crew, who rushed to set up. In seconds the whole thing was underway. "Rolling here," the cameraman said. "Speed here," the sound man added. And Steward, gazing directly into the camera, sucked in his fat and announced, "We're here at Goldmill's Gym, a Philadelphia landmark of sorts since 1929. The stench of toil permeates every corner. The sweat, a trademark of a unique profession. Yet the most unique feature is an unprecedented 50-to-1 underdog heavyweight named Rocky Balboa."

The camera turned to Rocky; the bright lights made him blink. It was like a silent inquisitor, sent to make Rocky blurt out all sorts of confessions. He felt as if it had caught him with his pants down and fifteen pimples on his ass. "Should I do this?" Rocky asked Mickey. Mickey nodded; he figured they shouldn't pass up the publicity—it was good for Goldmill's Gym, too. Rocky faced the glaring lights once again.

"So much has happened lately. Has it changed your life style much?" The reporter wanted to hear that the Rock had bought some custom-made suits and shirts, bought a Lincoln, hired a bodyguard to keep the women away from him, and so forth —the American success story—but Rocky, without guile, and much too honest to tell a lie, said, "People talk to me more."

"How're you preparing for this bicentennial bout?" Steward continued, hoping for something at least more detailed.

Rocky, who could not restrain himself, shouted,

"Hey, ya mother ever have any kids that lived, Fat Boy?" The gym exploded with laughter.

Flushed and scared, Steward almost whined, "We can cut that out later. Now, Rocky, please —Apollo Creed says that he'll let you stay three rounds before he puts you away."

Still painfully honest, Rocky replied, "You're a pig, a scumbag—but Apollo's a great fighter."

Steward was now terrified and was fast losing control of his bladder. "Do you feel you have a chance?" Steward gulped; he couldn't quite spit it out.

"Apologize for the cheap shot on TV."

". . . I was just making it colorful, Rocky," Stew whined.

"Apologize or I'll make your eye colorful."

". . . I'm very sorry."

"Maybe." He faced Mickey. Mickey whispered in his ear to go easy on the frightened reporter.

"Now you can ask one question," Rocky said.

"Do you have anything derogatory to say about the champion?" Steward whispered.

"Yeah, he's great." That was as derogatory as the Rock could get.

At that moment Apollo Creed and his entourage entered the gym, with Apollo bellowing, "I am the champion of the whole world!" He was wearing a white leather coat lined in sable. He not only looked like the champion of the whole world, he looked like a black god. So fashionable a picture did he make that the whole gym froze at the sight of him. Everyone turned and stared in wonderment. Mickey Goldmill shook his head in disbelief: He realized at last that it was a publicity stunt.

Walking over to Rocky, standing nose to nose, Creed declared, "Italian Stallion, I come over to tell you to be very smart an' after this fight donate what's gonna be left of your body to science, 'cause after this fight what's left won't fill a tuna-fish can! So beware, *mon cher!*" Rocky was speechless. Apollo turned to the cameras: "This classic fight— tha's right—this bicentennial fight's goin' down in the history books 'cause January first I'm gonna be the first man to bounce another man offa the planet Pluto!"

Dipper, enraged by the attention Rocky was getting, fumed at the far end of the ring; he could feel hate uncoiling in him like a snake about to strike.

Apollo Creed adopted a serious pose. "Now I got a special announcement, y'hear. For the first time in a lotta years this championship fight is gonna be on your home TV. Free—'course, that's just for Philly—my present to the city. Now some ya'll ain't much on likin' me, but ya gotta admit Apollo Creed is one *damn* generous, one hundred percent pure, government-inspected, Afro-American Folk Hero!"

Everyone laughed, but Dipper moved across the room, gliding, tense, brushing people aside. He stepped behind Rocky, nudging him. Rocky thought it was an accident and ignored him. Dipper pushed harder, and then Rocky glanced questioningly at him.

As loud as he could, Dipper said, "Ya' nothin', boy!"

Apollo stopped his sales pitch in mid-sentence; the television crew faced Dipper. And Dipper continued: "I say ya' nothin'!"

Mickey, aware of a weird situation that was in danger of becoming ugly, said, "What's happening here?"

"I'm happenin'!" Dipper challenged. "This mudder-fuckin' pig is takin' my shot. *I* iz a contender. He's nothin'."

Rocky, dumbstruck, gasped, "Yo, Dipper, why're ya ..."

Dipper shook his fist at Rocky. "Spar me in front of these mudderfuckin' TV dudes—I knock ya' ass to Jersey."

Dipper's fat black trainer held out his hands, and Dipper slapped them soul-style.

Again Mickey stepped in. "You can forget about sparring, kid."

"Yo' know I iz the nigger here! Yo' said so youself."

Almost apologetically, Mickey said to the crew, "Why let Rocky here take a chance on cuttin' or breakin' a hand? Take a shower, Dipper."

But Dipper wasn't going to be soft-talked into a shower to cool off. "Don't mouth me, old man, I'll knock yo' out too. C'mon, wop, spar me, let everybody see who's got the heat around here."

Silence loomed over the gym. Everyone realized that Dipper was out of control. Even Apollo became apprehensive: His light and lively humorous touch was being given the lead axe. The scene was too real. The frightened television crew slyly began putting away their expensive equipment.

Insanely, irrationally, Dipper continued. "Man, yo' best keep them cameras out! Fight me, boy! Let Creed here see the kind of punk he's fightin'."

Mike forced his way through the crowd and

stood behind Rocky. "Don't chance it, man. He's sick."

"This is gettin' out of hand," Mickey said angrily. "Rocky will fight in the ring January first, not here!"

"Yo' yellow, old man," Dipper hissed, dancing rings around himself and feinting into the smoky air.

"Not yellow, cautious." Then to the crew, "See, it's very easy for a fighter to accidentally hurt . . ."

Dipper suddenly stepped forward and slapped Rocky very hard across the side of the head. The gym became stone cold. Dipper was in total command and enjoying every moment of it. "If yo' afraid to fight me, then get down an' kiss my mudderfuckin' feet, boy."

Mickey looked around nervously; he knew it would be only seconds before the blood ran. Rocky stood motionless. "Let's take a walk, Rock," Mickey said. "Please, don't take a chance. He wants to hurt you so you can't fight."

Rocky swallowed his pride. He still had the string around his ankles. He started to shuffle away with Mickey. Dipper stepped forward and viciously slapped Rocky again. Mike jumped forward and stood in front of Dipper. "Why you tryin' to cut 'im, man! Back off, scumbag, or I'll bite your face!"

Dipper cut loose with a hook and knocked Mike flat. The room fairly reeked of fear. Apollo's eyes flicked back and forth between Rocky and Dipper. Apollo tapped his bodyguards, and they began to ease away.

"Now, pussy, kiss my feet," Dipper haughtily ordered.

Rocky eyed his friend lying on the floor. He shuffled forward and stood in front of Dipper.

Continuing almost in a whisper, Dipper repeated the last phrase, "Kiss 'em."

Rocky looked at Mickey, then lowered his eyes to Dipper's feet. They were firmly planted sweating in a size thirteen black boxing shoe, and ready to be kissed, or stepped on. Rocky started to bend toward the shoes. Without warning, he exploded with a pair of combinations into Dipper's exposed ribs. A crack was heard, and Dipper sank to the floor, writhing in pain. The room was silent except for Dipper's moaning. The gym had become a very gloomy place. Apollo Creed was stunned by the scene; in an instant he had viewed the raw passion of despair, hate, madness, retaliation, and defeat—the very opposite of the way he worked, with the detached cool of a heavy professional. He eyed Rocky with admiration and a hint of apprehension, then left without looking back. Mickey was the first one to shake off the chill. He shook his fists at the reporters and put his arm around Rocky, as if to say, "Here's a champ, not a chump!"

"The kid's got cannons—print that," he said with assurance.

The crowd dispersed, leaving a pathetic and broken figure lying on the dirty gym floor. Luckily it wasn't the Rock.

The telegrams were piling up like snow. Rocky scooped a handful up and tossed them aside. He was home, nice and cozy with his girl Adrian. "Don't you open them any more?" she asked.

"They either say, 'Kill the nigger,' or 'Hope you

die, Honky.' What ya got in the bag?" He kicked another pile of telegrams that were lying near the door, and they fell in a wide arc, coming to rest in a disordered, cantilevered bunch.

Adrian went to the window. She pulled a pair of short, colorful curtains from a shopping bag. They practically glared in the dark room. "Like?" Adrian asked proudly.

"Sharp, real sharp, real nice," Rocky answered. Certainly the curtains were an improvement on the dirty window shades that only came halfway down anyway.

"Really, you don't think they're overly feminine?" She wanted him to be pleased.

Rocky, as if considering a decision of great import, said: "No—sharp. You look great."

Adrian smiled and pulled out a small Christmas wreath. Rocky responded with a look of such love and warmth for her that she came and let him hold her in his arms.

"Adrian, you really look great, y'know. But I can't fool around durin' trainin'—makes the legs weak." He wanted Adrian there and now, in spite of his legs.

"Don't want weak legs," Adrian said, her lips flush against his.

"Can't fool around." He stepped away, not too far, and looked at her as if she were a masterpiece. "You look very great."

"The legs!" Adrian warned.

"Yeah. But I think weak legs ain't bad sometimes, y'know."

Adrian uncharacteristically removed her sweater, as Rocky moved toward her for another embrace.

Underneath her sweater was a T-shirt that read,
WIN, ROCKY, WIN.

"I thought it might be cute," she said shyly.

"Ya' right. Mebbe we best just hold hands—
the shirt made me feel guilty, y'know." And Rocky
laughed a good-natured, happy-to-be-alive-and-
well-in-Philadelphia laugh.

7

ONE PREDAWN IS like the next—gloomy, lonely, a kind of limbo in which the ghosts of yesterday linger like a haunting refrain. At this time of day, Rocky was already out running, and for extra weight he carried his huge dog Butkus. The dog didn't like this, of course; he wanted to be on all fours, running alongside Rocky. After half a block, Rocky sagged under the weight, and laughing, he began to wrestle with the dog on the pavement. Then playing hide-and-seek, Rocky tried to sneak away from the dog, but after a few steps the beast saw him and chased him down the street.

As usual Rocky jogged to the meathouse, this time followed by his new, faithful companion, Butkus. He stopped short when he noticed several television vans parked out front. He and the dog entered the freezer area and saw several reporters and men with minicameras milling around. Paulie was waiting for him. Rocky was upset, and went outside. Paulie followed.

"Yo, Rock. I made a few phone calls, an' thanks to me ya goin' to be a big man. Thatta dog?"

"It ain't a lobster," Rocky cracked. "Whatta these guys want?"

"To see ya train," Paulie answered proudly; he fancied himself a PR man.

Rocky was pissed off. "Yo, what's with you? It was supposed to be private."

"I thought I was doin' ya a favor. C'mon inside. Y'know, my sister really likes ya."

Rocky followed Paulie inside again. The whole thing was confusing, one interview after another when he least expected it; next thing he knew, the television crew would be setting up at his bathroom, waiting for him to take a crap.

A beautiful black woman reporter pointed in Rocky's direction, and suddenly he was surrounded and led into the freezer area, like a ship trapped in ice being rescued by a troupe of penguins. They pulled at him and positioned him beside a slab of hanging beef. The camera lights went on. For one hysterical moment, Rocky thought of doing a funny bit: pointing to the dead slab of beef and denying that he had murdered it, that yes, indeed, it did resemble his father, but that his father had died of natural causes.

The commentator, Diane Lewis, spoke soothingly. "Just relax, Mr. Balboa." Then he faced the camera, "Today we're here with the heavyweight challenger Rocky Balboa. The reason we're standing in a refrigerator box is that Mr. Balboa has an unusual method of training, and in a moment he is going to demonstrate it for our viewing audience. But first, Rocky, how did you ever come to train in an icebox?"

"Ah . . . my buddy Paulie let me in one day, an' I hit the beef here an' liked it. An' since I become a challenger, the owner don't mind neither." Rocky smiled sheepishly. He was relaxing. He was the challenger. And naturally, anyone interested in fights would want to know everything about him. He could feel self-assurance coming over him, warming him like a hot rum toddy.

"Is this a common training method—I mean, do other fighters pound raw meat?" Diane Lewis asked by rote.

"I think me an' Paulie invented it," Rocky answered pontifically. It was as if he were being asked how he discovered radium or the theory of relativity. It didn't occur to him that often, in the ring, it was raw meat that was being pounded, raw meat that felt every punch.

"Would you give us a demonstration?" the commentator requested.

Rocky stepped over to a hanging beef and began pounding with incredible intensity. Everyone present was taken aback. Rocky finished hitting the meat and stood there with his hands dripping blood: a primitive spectacle, a gladiator who could and would rip out his aggressor's guts with his bare hands. Rocky looked straight into the camera's lens and held up his bloody fists.

Unnerved, Diane Lewis bit her lips. She could taste a trickle of blood with the lipstick that had come off. "This is Diane Lewis in the meathouse with the southpaw, Rocky Balboa . . ."

Apollo Creed sat behind Jergens' desk with four middle-aged types discussing the forms and charts with Apollo's lawyer. Jergens was out somewhere attending to business, maybe making sure the arena had all the toilet paper, paper cups, soap, et cetera, for the night of the big match. And what were all those charts and forms? They were big money mapping our Creed's take from TV, radio, and so forth.

"How much is being channeled into West Coast closed-circuit advertising?" Creed asked.

"Conservatively, three hundred thousand," a lawyer said.

"Well, make it four hundred an' fifty—used to be my lucky number." Then turning to another lawyer, he said, "Send two hundred roses to the mayor's wife from me, get a picture, an' make sure it gets in all the papers."

The lawyer, trying to live up to the occasion, and being a smart-ass, asked, "What color roses, Apollo? An' what if the mayor's wife is allergic to roses?"

Apollo looked at him as if he were a living turd. "If she's allergic, I'll pay for the doctor afterward, but make sure she takes the picture first!"

A businessman interjected, "Long-stemmed roses, that's the only kind to get," then, "Do you want to run the fifteen radio spots in the Midwest? I think you could spend the money better in Canadian publicity."

"Yeah, I'd like to get Canada . . . see, if we can get a tax break . . . gimme the figures on the program concession." Apollo was brisk and businesslike; the circus was out there, but in here the real stuff was taking place.

Meanwhile, the trainer sat across the room in a darkened corner looking at a small television. He was watching Rocky's bloody exhibition on the news. He waved at Apollo. "Apollo, you oughta come see this boy you're gonna fight on TV. Looks like he means business."

But Apollo was too engrossed in his paperwork to be worried about anything else. "I mean business, too." He turned to the businessman nearest him and said, "The gross rental of the arena is gonna include the four hundred ushers, right? Gimme some coffee."

Still mumbling about how you have to watch out for bums, especially bums who don't seem to feel any pain, the trainer left the office to find a coffee shop and bring back some java.

Hey, where did the moon go? Meaning that it was a moonless night, but it didn't make any difference because there were street lamps and lighted windows to help the weary traveler on his murky way. Paulie, his blood containing a high concentration of alcohol, staggered up the stairs to his apartment. Fell up them would be more accurate. He went in, removed his coat, threw it on a chair, rubbed his red eyes, making them redder, and swayed into the kitchen. He took a bottle of wine out of the icebox, and as he swilled some down, he heard the sound of Rocky and Adrian's voices traveling from his sister's room. Paulie's face tightened, and he staggered toward the bedroom. Like a naughty child, or a dirty old voyeur, he stood outside the bedroom door and peered through a crack. What he saw was an innocent scene of flaccid domesticity: Rocky, Adrian, and the dog were watching TV in the darkened room. Adrian was speaking.

". . . and he called the reporters," she said, obviously speaking about Paulie.

"Yeah. Threw my whole day off," Rocky complained, an edge of anger in his voice.

"Don't be mad at him. He just wants to help."

"Yo, I ain't mad," Rocky explained, "I'm just outta joint when reporters are around. They take cheap shots, an' Paulie knows it."

"Are you going to say anything to him?" Adrian asked.

"What's to say? I dunno what he wants from me."

Filled with uncontrollable anger, Paulie smashed into the room. "Nothin'! I want nothin' from you!"

Shocked out of ten years' growth by her brother, who looked as if he were possessed, Adrian sought to exorcise his demon by saying his name out loud. "Paulie!" she shouted.

But he wouldn't be calmed down; though his tongue was as thick as pea soup and his eyes as red as ketchup, he flapped around the room squawking and making devilish jabs at the air. "Shut up! I want nothin'. I ain't no charity case! Get outta my house!"

"It's not your house," Adrian stated flatly.

Turning to Rocky, Paulie excommunicated him: "You ain't no friend no more. Go home! Outta my house I want ya!"

Embarrassed for Paulie and for Rocky, Adrian said, "Don't talk that way to him!"

"Get outta my life, both of ya," was Paulie's answer. He kicked the door out of frustration and appeared to be bordering on a nervous breakdown. "Outta my house I want ya!"

A little too reasonably, Rocky said, "It's cold outside, Paulie."

He had miscalculated the rage in Paulie, who went to the living room closet and removed a baseball bat. Rocky and Adrian quickly followed.

"I don't want ya messin' up my sister no more. He's scum from the corner. I didn't raise ya to hang with no bum!"

Adrian was speechless. Even if she had a speech she would have swallowed it. Rocky moved cautiously toward Paulie; a baseball bat in the hands of an amateur maniac could do more damage than the fists of a professional fighter.

Paulie raised the bat high, in a dangerously accurate position, where, if he wanted to, he could mash Rocky's face in. "Wanna hit on me? C'mon . . . c'mon, I'll break both ya' arms so's they never work."

Rocky became a statue. Only the beating of his heart through his shirt revealed his emotions.

Adrian cried, "Paulie! Stop now!"

Paulie stuck to his guns. "I want 'im outta here." Then turning to Rocky, he said, "Don't think I'm good enough to work for Gazzo?" He spit on the floor to show his disgust for all of those who would have liked to spit on him. "That's what I think of bums like you an' Gazzo!" He spit again for emphasis. "You're goin' up an' don't care enough to throw Paulie some crumbs!" He spit again, just out of habit. "I give ya meat, an' I give ya my sister, too!"

"Only a pig would say that!" Adrian shouted.

Paulie smashed a small table with the bat. A big table would have taken him longer to demolish, and longer to replace. Even though he was drunk, he chose his target carefully. "You forget what I went through to give ya the best," he said to Adrian. His voice was softening, like forgotten butter on the kitchen table.

Adrian didn't buy it. "You gave me what?! Knots! You gave me knots in here every day. You made me scared of everything!"

Paulie, combining the qualities of a mother hen and the bad fairy, said: "I always seen ya had the best, but did ya ever think of puttin' in a good word for me with this scumbag?" Unable to contain his rage, Paulie took another piece of furniture with him, this time a large lamp that he smashed to smithereens with the bat.

"Don't do that again!" Adrian ordered.

"Get away from me. I could never even get married 'cause you couldn't live by yourself . . . ya'd die by ya'self. So instead I put you two together. Did ya think of puttin' in a good word for me? *Ya owe me!*"

"Owe you what?" Adrian asked aggressively.

"Ya owe me an' are supposed to treat me *good!*"

"Good? Good, Paulie?! I've been treatin' you like a baby since I can't remember, it's so long. I'm the only one who feeds you an' puts you in bed when you can't stand up. And it's you that made me feel like a loser. That's what you used to call me—'loser.' What kind of name is that? So can ya blame me for not remembering to talk about you when I'm with Rocky. I don't owe you, Paulie, you owe me."

Paulie flared up and threatened Adrian with the bat. His small mind was working overtime; somewhere in its dim recesses he was still concerned about his sister's morals, and the Catholic code

that demanded she remain a virgin till marriage:
"You busted?" he said.

"What?" Adrian couldn't make out what he
meant.

"You a virgin? Ya let 'im in ya' pants, didn't
ya! Ya pulled down ya' pants an' let him have it,
didn't ya." Paulie was obviously hung on imagin-
ing the details of his sister's first time.

Mortified, Adrian ran to her room. Rocky advanced toward Paulie. It was about time. He was
fuming; his entire body was a smoke funnel for the
release of repressed anger. "Hey!" he said.

Paulie cocked the bat back and tensed. Rocky
remained still.

"I can't haul meat no more," he said softly.

"What can I do about it?" asked Rocky just as
softly.

"Christ, I been beggin' ya for a break until I'm
sick inside." Now Paulie was talking.

"What break? Huh? What break? Who am I to
give breaks." He thumped his chest for emphasis.
"I'm a fighter, you haul meat. You do what you
do, an' I do what I do best. That's it. That's life,
man!"

Rocky's remarks shamed Paulie, especially when
he said, "That's life, man!"

Rocky walked away from him, then returned.

"An' what ya said to my girlfriend ain't right.
Do it again, I'll kill ya." Now he was cooking. Putting Paulie straight. He went into the bedroom,
where he found Adrian with her face in the pillow.
She was rocking slightly. Rocky cradled her and
kissed her cheek.

"What a roommate," she said.

". . . Absolutely."

8

It was time to study Apollo Creed's every move —his style in the ring, his weak points—so Mickey and Rocky sat in Mickey's stuffy little office above the gym watching 8mm movies of Creed in action.

"His defense is great, can't lie 'bout that. You have a rollin' style. Can't retreat as fast. But your style ain't retreatin'," Mickey said. He stared at the flickering image, watching the black champ move across the screen like a huge dancer. "See how he plays sometimes . . . drives his cornermen nuts. Nobody knows his next move, him included. Now look, Creed's got the competition helpless against the ropes. Killer instinct. Ya both got the killer touch. Interestin'. See that! Right-cross combination. Beautiful. But you got the power to rip the body."

They watched more action, figuring out how to approach the fistic problem.

Mickey continued. "Rocky, when ya climb into the square, an' know ya' meetin' the best fighter in

the world, ya' gonna be ready. Ya' gonna be ready
'cause I been waitin' for fifty years. Fifty years.
When I'm done with ya, ya' gonna be able to spit
nails. Ya' gonna be able to eat lightnin' an' crap
thunder. Ya'll be a very, very dangerous person."

Rocky stared transfixed at the screen. He could
hardly wait to get in there with the champ and mix
it up.

"Put ya' whole body into it!" Mickey instructed.
"That ain't a bag, that's Creed, that's the mountain
that won't be moved. Hit 'im, hit 'im!"

Rocky pounded the heavy bag with intense concentration. He hit the rough canvas with all he
had, and from every angle, till his gloves felt like
bricks, and his arms as weak as a baby's. From the
bag he went to the slant board. It was almost per-
pendicular. While he did his sit-ups, he pounded
himself in the stomach with a dumbbell. His face
showed that he was in pain. After four sets of fifty
situps, Rocky did push-ups between two chairs, as
Mike sat on his shoulders, adding over a hundred
and fifty pounds of weight to deal with.

"Two more times! Ya can do it!" Mickey urged,
driving him on.

Later, Mike put on a pair of target gloves, and
Rocky moved around the ring swinging at them.
He grunted with every punch, blowing air out of
his mouth. Then, drenched in sweat, he made the
speed bag hum. Its rhythm was so perfect and
steady, with a number of interesting combinations,
that a symphony could have been written behind
it; "Ode to Goldmill's Gym." Rocky's face now
had a hard expression, and his complexion was
flushed. Mickey clicked a stopwatch, and pleased

with the way things were going, he patted Rocky's shoulders. He was very happy.

Rocky had just completed exercising with the medicine ball and was heading for the steam room when a thick man crossed the gym, and Mickey nodded. "Whatcha say, Al. Meet the Rock." Then to Rocky, "This is our cut man, Al Silvanni."

"Yo, Al," Rocky said. Al could be the most important man in Rocky's corner; a cut over Rocky's eye might blind him with dripping blood, and the fight would be over.

"Check the eyes, Al," Mickey said.

Al checked the skin around Rocky's eyes.

"Ain't bad. Seen worse. Cover up an' things'll be okay," Al remarked.

"Take a shower," Mickey ordered. "Ya' coolin' off too fast."

Heading toward the shower, Rocky was intercepted by Paulie. He stopped Rocky at the shower-room entrance.

"Yo, Rock, I think I found an angle to make some bread usin' ya name, ya mind?" he asked.

Exhausted, Rocky studied Paulie's face a moment and nodded that it was okay. He didn't have the heart to turn Paulie down, and he was too tired to ask what Paulie's scheme was. He swayed into the shower room, and Paulie strode off.

After the shower, Rocky felt great. A marvelous sense of well-being filled him. And in the street, young boys trailed him when he left the gym, proud to be in the company of the contender. He began to run, and they trailed him: He was the Pied Piper of Philadelphia, and all the little mice came squeaking and scampering behind him to the very edge of night.

In the twilight, Rocky found himself alone at the very bottom of a huge flight of steps that seemed to stretch to the heavens. He took a deep breath and sprinted up the never-ending stairs. Halfway up, he felt the strain, but he kept going, and nearing the top he pumped with all his strength and reached his goal. He looked down the steep stairs and swelled with pride. He was ready. He could take the world on. But the world would have to wait—Apollo Creed came first.

The mayor wanted to see Rocky. It made him very nervous. People in authority had always bothered him, made him feel small, like a kid asking for favors that would be refused. Rocky was only sure of himself when he could hit, beat a target into the ground—a human target—then looming above it, he'd become omnipotent, a giant destroying all those who stood in his path. His father had been a big man, a punishing man, the Colossus of Rhodes with four extra arms and a terrible voice that bounced itself off walls without breaking. And his mother whispered.

Mayor Rizzo's aide led Rocky into the official office. It was almost bare except for a wide pine desk and two chairs. The mayor sat comfortably behind his desk.

"Sit down, Rocky," the mayor said. It seemed odd to Rocky that the mayor knew his name, even though he had Rocky's name on the papers in front of him and had invited him by name. Still, it made Rocky uncomfortable—his name in the mouth of an important person, a public personality, someone he had known through newspaper articles and TV, a fictitous person who in a way didn't exist in the flesh.

The mayor opened a thick file that lay in front of him. "I've been going over your record. You've been the busy type." He continued reading, "Nineteen arrests, probation three times, expelled from seven public schools in 1964 and '65."

Rocky tried to disappear into the chair upholstery. His record—that was the person he used to be, the kid taking because nobody would give. There were the haves and the have-nots. He had been the latter, without love and without things, so the things became a substitute for love. And the things he chose to steal were TVs, clock radios, cameras—possessions any American worth his salt would want to own, imagined he needed, had to have. In a way Rocky had been trying to say he was just like everyone else, but he had gone about it the wrong way. What he did get in the short run was a lot of attention—and a record. The record would stay long after his change, a reminder that he had been a bad egg, a loser, someone outside of society.

The mayor continued. "I'm a very busy man, but I just wanted to remind you that you'll be setting an example for thousands of guys like yourself, and maybe start them off in a new direction and give our police force a break. I also hope you try your very best and bring pride to Philadelphia."

Rocky had used them, and now they were going to profit from it. Still, he had pride in having come through. If his story could help other young punks, he was willing to tell his story, set an example. It would be as if he were going back and helping himself. Only someone who had been there could know what it was like.

He simply said, "I'll try."

The mayor pressed a button, and a photographer entered. Turning to Rocky, he asked, "Would you stand up, please?"

Rocky rose, and the mayor shook his hand. It was a thick hand, with manicured nails, that lay in Rocky's weathered palm. Their picture was taken three times. Rocky didn't change his expression. It was serious and intelligent with the importance of the occasion. The reporter left.

"Thank you for coming by, Rocky. Good luck," Mayor Rizzo said earnestly.

"Any time," Rocky magnanimously replied. The rigors of celebrity were becoming easier for him—could become second nature, even a pleasure. This was the land of opportunity where scrounging could become lounging, and longing for the pot of gold at the end of the rainbow a reality. It didn't really matter where a person began; what mattered was how he ended.

"Wait," the mayor said, sitting down again behind the solid protection of his desk. "After the fight you'll have nearly a hundred and fifty thousand dollars. What do you plan to do with it?"

"I'm not sure."

"You must have some idea."

" . . . I dunno maybe run for mayor."

At first the mayor was shocked, but then he broke into a big, friendly laugh and Rocky left after shaking hands again.

9

STREWN ON THE kitchen table in Rocky's apartment
were a few of his scrapbooks containing items from
Newsweek—headline: "The Italian Stallion or
Donkey?"—*Sports Illustrated, The American
Sportsman, Ring Magazine, World Boxing, True,
Philadelphia Magazine* showing Rocky standing,
shaking hands with the mayor, and a multitude of
other clippings.

Adrian shook her head admiringly as she looked
through one of the scrapbooks. "Rocky, do you
realize everybody in this country knows your face,
and after the fight everybody in the world is going
to!"

"Yeah," Rocky responded. He wasn't sure he
wanted everyone in the world to know his face;
that would get to be a hassle. He'd have to hire
bodyguards to keep the crowds away just as if he
were Jackie Onassis, or Richard Burton. He
wouldn't be able to take an ordinary walk, or eat a
hoagie without being stared at.

The new telephone on the wall rang; it was white
and had push buttons instead of a dial. "My first
call," Rocky said to Adrian; then, "Who is this?
Bruce? Bruce who? Yo, Bruce! How ya been? I
ain't seen ya for nine or eight years. . . . Yeah,
things is great, how's things with you upstate? Ya
sellin' real estate? . . . Hey, that's a good job. . . .
Yeah, I got an advance, but I bought ringside seats
for the guys at the gym. I get the hundred an' fifty
grand after the fight. . . . Yeah, I know it's a lotta
money. . . . Condominiums? Nobody uses them any
more. Listen, I think a pet shop is a good in-
vestment, y'know. . . . I don't care 'bout long
hours. . . . There's no depreciation . . . that don't
matter none to me. . . . Yeah, I like animals. Why
don't ya give me ya' number an' I'll call ya back?
Lemme get a pencil."

Rocky pretended to get a pencil.

"Okay," he continued, "what is it . . . 412-659-
2424. Yeah, yeah, thanks for callin'. . . . Sure I'll
get back to ya, Bruce. See ya." Rocky hung up.

"What was that you said about a pet shop?"
Adrian asked sweetly.

"What?" Rocky asked. His mind was already in
a distant place.

"What did you say about a pet shop?" Adrian
insisted.

"I don't want ya cleanin' nobody else's cages no
more," Rocky explained. He sounded preoccupied.

"Is everything all right?" Adrian asked solicitously.

"I gotta go out for a while," was all the answer
she got.

Rocky grabbed his coat and moved to the front
door. He turned to Butkus. "Come."

Rocky arrived at Goldmill's Gym. He had the key to the door. Everyone else had gone home. Rocky moved across the gym through eerie shadows, the dog trotting by his side. He moved up the steps to Mickey's office. At the top of the stairs he looked down at the ring, reflected for a moment, then entered the office. After turning on the lights, he quickly cleaned the cluttered desk and set up the projector. He went to the cabinet and removed a stack of 16mm films.

Several hours later, Rocky was deeply engrossed in watching another Apollo Creed film. He was sitting motionless when suddenly he bolted upright. Something had caught his eye. He sprang at the projector and reran the scene several times. Rocky hardly noticed time passing; he was searching for something in Creed's style, his Achilles heel, so to speak. Suddenly, as Apollo was delivering a knockout blow to an unfortunate opponent, Rocky stopped the projector. Rocky moved right up to freeze frame and inspected it like it was a priceless painting. Then he backed off and began writing on a note pad.

The first light of dawn streamed through Mickey's filthy windows. Rocky had had all he could take; he was slumped in the chair and had lost all interest in observing Apollo Creed on film. The film had just completed its run through the projector and lazily flopped around the top reel. Listlessly, Rocky rubbed his reddened eyes.

Mickey opened the door and found him there. The two men stared at each other for a long moment. Mickey studied Rocky's despondent expression and knew what was on the fighter's mind.

"I know what you're thinkin', kid. At least ya got a shot. All ya can do is try ya' best."

Rocky stood up but didn't say a word; he was dead tired and discouraged. He was beginning to realize that he would have to actually appear in the ring with the champ, and thereby become over two hundred pounds of mincemeat! He wondered whether it was so important to get your shot. Maybe it was better to imagine how it would have been. Rocky inched past Mickey and left the room with Butkus. Mickey walked over to the projector. He idly pushed the machine with a lazy motion until it slid off the desk and crashed to the floor.

After leaving Mickey's gym, Rocky and his dog moved down the street listlessly and headed for home. It was daylight when he arrived. Adrian was asleep on the couch. He lowered himself beside her. Her eyes opened.

"Can't do it," Rocky said.

"What?" Adrian askd.

"I can't beat him."

"Apollo?" She took his cold hand and warmed it between her palms. Rocky moved close to her. He needed comfort.

"Yeah, I can't beat him," Rocky said sadly.

Adrian touched his face. She loved every line, every pore. If she could have, she would have given him super strength to beat Apollo Creed. Her touch made him less anxious. He opened up a bit.

"I been watchin' the movies . . . studyin'. He ain't weak nowhere," he said with emphasis.

"What're we goin' to do?" Adrian asked, as if she were going to be in the ring with him, fighting alongside him, taking and giving punishment. In a way she would be there, the invisible helpmate, the spirit of true love. "Oh, Rocky, you worked so hard."

"It ain't so bad, 'cause I was a nothin' before."

"Don't say that."

"C'mon, it's true. But that don't bother me—I just wanna prove somethin'. I ain't no bum. It don't matter if I lose, don't matter if he opens my head. The only thing I wanna do is go the distance, that's all. Nobody's ever gone fifteen rounds with Creed. If I go them fifteen rounds an' that bell rings an' I'm still standin' I'm gonna know then I weren't just another bum from the neighborhood."

He gently lowered himself beside Adrian.

10

IT WAS THE horrible or wonderful night, whichever way you want to look at it, of the bicentennial fight, and the Philadelphia Spectrum was filled to capacity. The cheap seats had filled fast, right from the first prelim, and the crowd was boisterous, in a holiday mood not unlike the spirit that infected watchers at a hanging—though no bets were laid there. At ringside, the celebrities and wealthy fight fans discussed the pros and cons of the championship match—how many rounds it might go, whether Rocky would be kayoed before he had danced a complete waltz around the ring, what Creed would do or say to antagonize his opponent. Very few had pity for Rocky; they figured the money would make up for the injury—and they were sure there would be some danger. Nearly everyone held a red, white, and blue streamer, and the arena was decorated in tons of patriotic red, white, and blue. High above the ring were huge posters of Apollo Creed and Rocky Balboa.

The silence in Creed's dressing room was earplug dead, except for some noise that filtered under the door from the arena. Apollo's hand was being taped, white and tight. The rasping sound of the adhesive tape was very pronounced. It said, "Use me correctly and you won't break any bones in your hand." Once Apollo had fought with a broken metacarpal in his right hand. It had hurt like hell and swollen up afterward, but he had won the fight. It took more than broken bones to finish him. It would take at least ten more years of fighting bums before he retired to the old "rockin' chair." The money was too good. He wasn't about to break his ass to earn a dollar. Let 'em come! He'd fight 'em, and he'd take home the million, while they picked up a hundred thousand or so in smaller denominations, and be glad of it.

The atmosphere in Rocky's dressing room was the same—dim, and quiet, with only the sound of Al wrapping Rocky's hand. Adrian watched in silence as Rocky's hand became a mummy, preserved within its traditional shroud. Again the most pronounced sound was the rasping of the adhesive tape.

As Rocky's other hand was taped, his breathing became heavier, more nervous, faster. Mickey put drops into Rocky's nose to keep it open, help him breathe. Then grease was smeared around his eyes, covering old scars that might open.

In Apollo's dressing room, the ceremony of blights was continuing just as in Rocky's dressing room: drops up the nostril to increase oxygen intake, heavy coating of vaseline ringing the eyes with a wet shine that made them look deeper, like a hole where the moon used to be, the wrapping to protect his other hand. Apollo's trainer dug his fingers deeply into the thick neck muscles of Apollo's upper back and neck. He then slipped a mouthpiece into Apollo's mouth. Apollo shook his head, and the trainer removed it and tried another one in the champ's mouth. Creed nodded yes.

In Rocky's tomblike dressing room, Al had wrapped his arms around Rocky's waist and was lifting his diaphragm up. It seemed to Rocky that his breath was actually roaring. He could hear it rushing through his ears, and the blood pounding. "S'cuse me," he said to Al, and made for the toilet. Once there, he got down on his knees and prayed.

"Dear God," he began, whispering, "I'm sorry to be asking ya a favor in this here toilet, but it's private, an' I know ya'll unnerstand. See, God, I don't wanna get killt, an' I don' wanna embarrass my girl an' my friends. So please, I'll nevah ask ya for anothah thing if ya'll let me go the distance. I know I ain't a winnah, that ain't in the cards—but I'm gonna try. Amen. Thank you, God." Completing the prayer. Rocky stood and looked at himself in the mirror. Suddenly a wave of emotion swept over him as he realized that in a very few moments he would face the most overwhelming challenge of his life. He walked out of the john as if he were leaving the royal throne room. He had managed to compose himself. A guard leaned in and nodded that it was time, then left.

"It's time, kid," Mickey said.

Rocky nodded and moved toward Adrian.

"I'll wait for you here," Adrian said and kissed him. Rocky left with his trainers. There are a few times that a man must go it alone, without loved ones, or anyone—when he faces death . . . and when he has to fight the odds, mano a mano.

Adrian was close to tears. She was allowed.

Rocky, Mickey, Mike and Al started down the long hallway. Up ahead were three security guards protecting the granite ribbon that led to the arena. All that was missing was the dolorous drumbeat that leads those sentenced to death to their final drop into eternity. It wasn't that bad. The trap door was stuck, and Rocky had both feet on the granite. Mickey and Al were bouncy, on their toes, Rocky had the flat-footed out-toe shuffle-step of a fighter; he just kept going straight ahead without grace, without haste, not even worried any more.

"Yo, Mick, can I have my robe?" Rocky asked.

He put on his robe; embroidered across the back in flaming letters was the motto,

THE ITALIAN STALLION

Pennzoil

Mickey was not amused. "Don't you care what the people will say? You're a contender, not a billboard!"

"I'm doin' it for a friend," Rocky said.

"Whatta you get outta this?" Mickey insisted, sure that Rocky had been taken.

"I get the robe, an' Paulie gets three grand," Rocky confessed.

"Shrewd," Mickey commented.

At ringside, reporters were already at their typewriters, TV commentators were making their preliminary comments in front of a panel of closed-circuit televisions, and the judges were fidgeting with newly sharpened pencils, restlessly waiting to make their marks on paper that would add up to "who won."

"Hello, I'm Bill Baldwin and on behalf of the Philadelphia Spectrum would like to welcome our viewing audience to the World Championship Bicentennial Heavyweight Fight, the first major event of the Bicentennial Year. A point of interest is that the fight is 'being beamed to more than seven hundred and fifty million fans in theaters in nearly every corner of the world. I would like to welcome an old friend and co-commentator for this evening's event . . . Jimmy Michaels," Baldwin said.

Michaels, as cool as a TV set that hasn't been turned on, picked up his cue and, smiling at the audience said, "Thank you, Bill. The electricity is everywhere tonight. Rocky Balboa, a fifty-to-one underdog, is living a Cinderella story that has captured people's imaginations all over the world. To quote a popular sport magazine, 'The fighting styles should be "The caveman against the cavalier." ' From the increase in sound it appears the challenger is now approaching the ring. His record is forty-four wins, twenty losses, and thirty-eight knockouts."

Commentator Bill Baldwin took his turn at the mike. "I only wonder if this man has the skill to get past three rounds. Vegas odds say no."

A wedge of uniformed guards knifed down the aisle to the ring. Many people wished Rocky well as he passed; he was like a life-size wooden saint whose elevated platform hadn't been built yet, so he was pushed and pulled down the aisle

in a manner too abrupt and rough for a saint.
Those who didn't wish him well hurled insults
at him; but who can be a saint and not be reviled
and insulted? Mickey, a stalwart at Rocky's side,
didn't hear the insults; he heard the general roar
of the crowd, and he was elated—from his face
one could tell that it was the greatest night of his
life. Rocky spotted familiar faces from the gym
but made no sign. From the back of the arena,
a superstupendous roar went up, as if the earth
were giving way: Apollo Creed had appeared;
he was in a mock boat and dressed like George
Washington, and he was throwing silver dollars
into the audience. This nearly created a panic
as people tried to catch and fight for the glitter-
ing silver discs. The noise built to deafening
proportions, and while some folks were still scram-
bling for the unexpected souvenir dole, Creed's
trainer held the rope and Creed bounded into
the ring. He tore off the Washington outfit, and
it was clear that under one outfit Creed was garbed
in another: an outrageous Uncle Sam costume.
On his head he wore a red, white, and blue
sequined top hat. The robe was a matching red,
white, and blue sequined number. His trunks were
red, white, and blue silk with stars around the
waistband. The boxing shoes matched the trunks.
On his chin was a pointed white Uncle Sam beard.

Baldwin reported, "You could go deaf with the
noise—it undoubtedly means champion Apollo
Creed is heading toward the ring . . ."

Hitting himself on the head with disbelief, the
other commentator screamed, "Am I seeing right?
Creed is approaching the ring in a boat. Is he
supposed to be George Washington? Obviously

so, going by pictures of Washington I've seen in the history books. I'd say close, but no cigar."

Officiously and officially, the other commentator reported, "It's been confirmed that it is definitely an impersonation of George Washington—a great way to start off 1976."

Immediately Creed began to dance gracefully in a wide circle. He passed within inches of Rocky. His Uncle Sam beard almost brushed Rocky's face. "I want you, I want you!" he taunted. The crowd loved it. Apollo Creed floated back to his corner.

"Don't let 'im get you tight," Mickey warned.

"Whatta ya think that outfit cost?" Rocky inquired. He hadn't taken the taunt personally; he had distanced himself and was merely an observer enjoying Creed as much as the crowd. It was like a Halloween party: Creed had knocked on his door yelling "Trick or treat"; Rocky hadn't prepared a treat for his costumed visitor, so he had to expect a trick, and Creed had a lot of tricks up his sleeve. Rocky would be ducking, but not for apples.

The announcer, who was none other than Miles Jergens himself, stepped to the center of the ring. Several men in suits stood against the ropes. Paulie was dressed nicely and sat at ringside with a pretty blond woman who was also dressed nicely. They were the nicely twins. Rocky waved at him. Paulie waved back and secretly gestured to his date: "Ain't she a beauty!" is what he meant. Rocky smiled and gestured back: "Not bad!"

"Ladies and gentlemen," the announcer broadcast, "welcome to the Bicentennial Heavyweight Championship fight. We are very proud to have

with us four former great champions . . . Ladies
and gents, the one and only 'Manassa Mauler'—
Jack Dempsey!" The crowd roared; crowds always roar, as if it takes thousands to make the
sound of one aroused animal. Jack Dempsey in a
striped brown double-breasted suit, looking old
and stocky, waved to the crowd and went to
Creed's corner.

"Good luck, kid," Dempsey said. "Someday
you'll own a restaurant, too—a soul food restaurant."

"Thanks, Jack. But you know, soul food is poor
people food; my people are movin' up to Porter-
house," Creed answered.

Dempsey moved off, approached Rocky, slapped
him on the back in a peremptory manner, and repeated his "Good luck, kid!" He climbed under the
ropes and took his seat.

"Christ, Jack Dempsey!" an amazed Rocky
said to Mickey.

A short time later, the announcer pointed and
the timekeeper rang the bell. This time the announcer introduced Jake La Motta, the man who
decided that he would not feel pain, and never
did, no matter who was hitting him. He had believed in psyching himself to stand the punishment; and it had worked, even against Bob
Satterfield, who had one of the most powerful
punches in fight history. Only thing about Satterfield, he had a glass jaw and was liable to be
knocked out himself. Sugar Ray Robinson had
mixed it up with La Motta quite a few times
and had won the middleweight title from him in
Chicago on St. Valentine's day in 1951. During

the sixth round, La Motta's arms tired of punching
and Sugar Ray did him in.

". . . Former middleweight champion, 'The
Bronx Bull'—Jake La Motta!" the announcer
shouted into the mike. Jake raised his fist and
gave best wishes to both contenders. He, too,
was short and stocky, and his voice had the
gravelly, slurred speech of an old fighter. Again
the bell, hardly a fanfare but appropriate, and
the announcer continued with his list of celebrities:
"The man with the big punch . . . everybody's
favorite, 'The Brown Bomber'—Joe Louis!"

Joe bowed and stepped to Creed's corner. Creed
struck a boxing pose, and Louis tossed a playful punch. It was delightful show biz, and the
crowd loved it. They had forgotten how the govern-
ment had dunned Joe for some huge sum for his
income tax, a sum that could never be earned
and repaid in one lifetime. Joe, for whom all
of Harlem had united and celebrated the night he
won the heavyweight championship . . . Joe, the
pride of black pride!

The announcer continued: "The man with the
big punch . . everybody's favorite, 'The Brown
Bomber'—Joe Louis!" and then realized that he
had just introduced Joe; it was just that his eye
had picked up the wrong line on the piece of
paper he held. Without batting an eyelash, he
corrected himself, "Now, last but certainly not
least . . . the former heavyweight champion, a son
of Philly—smoking Joe Frazier!"

Frazier rumbled to the center of the ring in
a bright green suit. The crowd cheered its own.
Apollo put on a show, stealing the thunder from
Frazier; he grimaced and gestured as if he were

going to attack him. His cornermen held him back. They could hardly restrain Apollo or their amusement. Frazier went to Rocky's corner. "Save some of him for me," he said.

As Frazier left the ring, the commentators at the TV cameras beckoned to him. "The former champ looks great . . . Can we get Joe over here? . . . Here he comes."

Joe Frazier stood in front of the commentators.

"Joe, what are your feelings about tonight's fight?" Bill Baldwin asked.

"Well, I think any man who works an' trains hard always got a chance," Joe answered.

"You look in great shape, Joe," commentator number two remarked.

"I'm always in shape!" Frazier retorted.

The timekeeper rang the bell, and the announcer began announcing the fight itself: "Now for the evening's main event. In the corner to my right, the challenger, wearing white trunks, at one hundred an' ninety-one pounds, one of Philly's own sons—'The Italian Stallion,' Rocky Balboa."

The crowd responded with good cheer and few boos. They were not about to bring down their own.

Then turning to Creed, the announcer continued: "In the far corner, wearing red, white, an' blue, weighing in at two hundred and ten pounds, undefeated in forty-six fights, the heavyweight champion of the world—'The Master of Disaster,' Apollo Creed!"

The arena exploded! And Creed put on a display of hand speed: flicking and darting at the air with poisonous snap.

The referee motioned to both fighters. They

stepped to the center of the ring. As the referee explained the rules, Apollo and Rocky stared hard into each other's eyes. The referee's voice faded, and the fighters' mean expressions almost had sound—the sound of thunder clapping over mountains, or the antlers of moose clashing in an age-old battle of heirarchies: something frightening and ancient was being communicated.

". . . Now come out fighting," the referee finished, as if they would have stood in their corners if he hadn't told them. It was as if they were going to be tried and had to be advised of their rights.

The fighters returned to their corners.

"God bless ya, Rock," Mickey said.

"Thank ya, Mick. I'm gonna try," Rocky said.

The bell rang. Creed danced forward and boxed Rocky as though he considered him an amateur.

Bill Baldwin reported: "The champ stings the slower challenger with jabs at will . . . Balboa blocks eighty percent of the blows with his face . . . Creed doesn't look the best he's ever been but is moving smoothly . . . Creed snaps out a triple combination that backs Balboa into a corner . . . oh, a solid hook by Creed, a master of fist-men."

Commentator Michaels was given the nod to continue, while Baldwin drank some of his cold black coffee. "The champion is smiling and toying with the man . . . trying to give the fans their money's worth and make a show of it with the badly outclassed challenger . . Creed is down!"

With a sudden explosion, Rocky had let go of a tremendous upswing to the jaw, and that was what had dropped Creed. The arena went wild.

Creed's eyes showed disbelief . . . and so did Rocky's. He backed into his corner. Mickey and Mike yelled at him: "You can do it! Goddammit, you got the power! The body, get the body!!! Ya got him goin'!"

The referee was counting: "Six. . . . Seven! . . . Eight! . . ."

Creed was up, his playful attitude gone. He was all business now. His lightning jab stung Rocky's face repeatedly. "Come at me, sucker!" Apollo taunted.

Rocky charged, and a terrific right crashed against Apollo's chin, followed by an uppercut to the liver that caused Creed to cringe. Apollo countered with jabs, and Rocky whipped brutal combinations to the body.

The bell came to the rescue.

In his corner, Rocky asked Mickey, "How'm I doin'?"

"Real good," Mickey answered.

"See how fast he is . . . damn!" Rocky was breathing hard, rinsing his mouth with water, letting his arms hang relaxed at his sides.

"Breathe deep. Keep ya chin down! Use the legs and drive through 'im. Attack . . . Attack . . . ! Attack!" Mickey advised.

Apollo Creed didn't even sit down in his corner.. He stood there facing out to the crowd, clowning around to prove that he wasn't hurt, but to his trainer, he whispered, "That boy damn near broke my arm."

"Sure. He can hit—don't play no more. Stick an' move, hear?"

Apollo layed it out. "I'll carry him till the third."

"Don't play with this man," the trainer cautioned. "He's fightin' hard. Let 'im feel some real heat."

The bell for the second round rang. Rocky rushed out fast and furious. Apollo pelted out a left hook that raised a goose egg over Rocky's eye. Apollo employed footwork that dazzled Rocky. He had class, no mistaking that. He studied Rocky and let loose with his lightning jab. It had cutting accuracy. Still, Rocky shuffled ahead, bombarding Creed's midsection with hooks.

The round ended with Apollo assaulting Rocky with blinding combinations and delivering a stupendous right cross that flung Rocky into the ropes and shattered his nose.

Again Apollo stood in his corner and joked with the fans, but he was beginning to show the strain from the body punches.

"Man, I rearranged his face with that right. The people love what's happenin' tonight," Apollo said to his trainer.

"People nothin', you in a fight, my man. Ya best believe what you hear: Knock that boy out soon an' let's go home."

Apollo was right: He had rearranged Rocky's face, and in Rocky's corner Mickey and Benny were both working on it to try to reduce the swelling around his eyes. His nose was really shattered. Rocky was having a hard time trying to breath.

"Ya nose is broke," Mickey observed sadly.

"Damn! How's it look?" Rocky asked.

"It's an improvement—Don't swallow the blood. Go for his ribs. Don't let 'im breathe." Mickey was upset about Rocky's broken nose, more than he let on: It was the beginning of the end.

"The guy's great," Rocky said in awe.

Really bugged by this remark, Mickey sassed Rocky. "Why don't ya tell 'im you're a fan!"

Commentator Michaels, caught up in the action, spoke rapidly into his microphone: "If you had asked anyone who knows boxing, they never would've predicted a first round knockdown and the second-round punishment to the body of the champion. Most fighters will tell you that receiving a good body punch is the next worse thing to dying."

"Round three ready to start," Baldwin continued, "and it should be interesting to see if Creed can put the challenger away . . . there goes the bell."

Round three. Apollo came out dancing. He skipped and sidestepped Rocky's sledgehammer hooks. An expert ring general, Apollo used the ring fully. Rocky kept tearing in, and Creed developed a swelling over one eye. Near the end of the round, Rocky fired a penetrating punch to the heart.

Down in the seats, cold beer was doing a brisk business, peanuts and popcorn ran second, and Breyer's cup of vanilla and chocolate ice cream was more popular with those who had begun with a foot-long hot dog. When there was a lot of action, there was a lot of eating; when the action slowed down, there were insults: "Hit 'im in the leg," "Open 'im up," "Step back an' stop dancin'," —and the classic "Kill the bum!" The commentators, eyes fastened on the fight, called every move with the enthusiasm of paid observers: "Apollo almost sprints out of his corner . . . feints and throws a pair of left-right combinations. Balboa drops beneath a left uppercut and lands a very solid shot on Creed's temple. Not much movement from Balboa . . . duck a left, a right, another left, and explodes with a right hook to the temple . . . I mean explodes! The champ backs off."

"There's no way Apollo expected this kind of hitting power," the other commentator added.

"No way," his friend agreed, "but the brilliant ability of the champion to master situations like this is one of his most outstanding traits . . . Creed tosses a perfect right hand that rocks Rocky . . . Creed on the offensive . . . Balboa takes the punishment and counters with a left flush over the heart . . . that hurt!"

The wallop knocked Apollo off balance. Rocky released a terrifying uppercut that opened a gash under Creed's eye. His face contorted with excruciation.

His trainer yelled, "Cover your face! Cover up! My man's cut, my man's bleedin' . . . Get ready!"

The bell sounded, and in Apollo's corner his men worked frantically to close the wound. The ring doctor inspected the cut.

"Bad? Talk to me, man!" the trainer said to the doctor.

"Deep, but passable." the doctor answered.

Apollo stared at Rocky. "That man's takin' his job too serious."

"He's movin' to your left, don't let him no more —dance and stick, hear? Don't play. I know what ya' feelin' but don't play."

Apollo answered, "He got lucky, man!"

"Luck! You fightin' a crazy man. But you got him hurt bad." Then to his assistant, "More ice, now!"

Rocky's face was in very bad shape, not cut but wretchedly swollen around the eyes.

"How you holdin' up, kid?" Mickey asked.

"Fine. That guy's great," Rocky answered with admiration.

"Gimme the water! Ya' gettin' tagged with his right. I think you should feint left and high hook 'im. Al, check the eyes! Can you see?" Mickey was observing Rocky very closely.

"See what?"

"Ya sappin' his strength. He's losin' steam."

"He ain't losin' nothin'," declared Rocky.

"Keep on him. You're doin' great," Mickey insisted.

In the next ten rounds Apollo cut and slashed Rocky to ribbons. He was so cut up he could have been hung from a maypole and braided. But Apollo paid dearly for the onslaught. Both his eyes and lips were cut, and there were welts across his mid-section attesting to Rocky's body-battering power.

During the early part of the fight, Adrian had been alone in Rocky's dressing room, but as the excitement of the crowd reached her ears, she couldn't stay put and was lured to the arena.

Stepping out of the dressing room, she walked down the corridor. The mounting cheers hurried her along. She opened the door at the end of the corridor and was hit by a thunderous wave of sound. The guard at the door turned for a moment to see who it was, but then went back to watching the fight.

Adrian stood at the rear of the arena and watched the battle. She was entranced by the power of it all; her heart beat faster and her blood pulsed.

Back in the ring, Rocky kept grinding ahead. He planted a thumping left over the champion's heart, and Creed winced. Rocky was game, but losing.

At ringside, Paulie was frantic, living the fight from his seat. Mr. Gazzo and his bodyguard watched from the second row; he could taste the sweat and blood staining the trunks of both contenders. Gazzo was proud of Rocky; he hadn't been too sure of the boy, even though he gave him some money. Now it was worth it. The bodyguard remained impassive; Rocky's good show only made him hate Rocky more. Gazzo leaned over and said proudly, "The Rock's got real stones."

Rocky ripped and tore into Creed's body. Creed countered with a ceaseless stream of rapierlike lefts. Both men were fighting with appalling tenacity, but the challenger was seriously outclassed.

"C'mon . . . Lemme cut ya!" ejaculated Apollo.

Rocky waded in, and Creed employed incredible footwork. He set himself and cut loose with a thunderbolt right cross to Rocky's already broken nose. Blood sprayed from the wound, and red droplets dripped from his chin. Rocky took a merciless beating and was staggered by a torrent of combinations. His eyes were closed, but Creed couldn't drop him. The bell rang, luckily. It had become a matter of survival—how to last each round, how to counter each brutal attack though bruised and bleeding. The sell-out crowd loved it. Even real blood seemed to be ketchup and the heavy thud of fists merely sound effects left over from a movie. The fight was real only to the contenders—the underdog and the man who already had his name etched in gold letters in boxing history.

The commentators could barely sit still: "Without a doubt, this is the most punishing brawl I have ever seen. The ringside audience is spotted with blood, they have had a transfusion of courage, they're polka-dotted with the signature of bravery: Red, red, red is the color of their main event. This fight should have been stopped rounds ago, but Rocky Balboa refuses to fall. . . Is he hero or fool?"

The other commentator continued, wiping some blood from the mike with a tissue, "Not only has Balboa refused to fall, but he has beaten the champion's body without mercy, and the bout has become a vicious slugfest. There is no joy in Fistville: This is a brawl, both battlers tireless . . . thrilling, simply thrilling!"

Apollo's corner was in a turmoil—the champion was definitely hurt

"My side," indicated Apollo.

"Get that doctor," the trainer said to his assistant.

"No doctor!" Apollo ordered.

"You're hurtin', man!" the trainer insisted.

"No doctor! I'm feelin' good, bro!" he lied. He could stand pain: that didn't matter. What he wanted to do was deck the Italian Stallion, put him out for the count and then some.

In Rocky's corner things were also frantic: After all, Rocky's eyes were swollen shut, and it would take a small operation to open them. Mickey wanted to know whether Rocky wanted to keep going. As a friend and adviser, he would have liked Rocky to throw in the towel.

"Wanna keep goin?" Mickey asked anxiously.

"Would you keep goin'?" Rocky asked.

"Yeah," Mickey answered, after thinking a while.

Mike interrupted with what seemed like an order. "No more, ya wanna lose an eye? No more!"

"Open my eyes . . . please, open my eyes!" Rocky pleaded.

Mickey nodded to Al, who secretly placed a small ring knife between his index and middle finger. In one smooth movement he dragged the razor over the blood welts and quickly covered the draining wounds with gauze. It was done so quickly that no one was aware of the operation.

At the rear of the arena, Adrian looked at the ring: she was transfixed, in a state of hypnotic hyperviewing. She was caught up in the heat of the battle that, because of its distance from her, was like a shrine for which two tiny muscled saints were battling.

Round fourteen was announced by the bell, the bell of the brawl, and Rocky bore in close. Apollo still had spring in his legs. He seemed determined to make round fourteen his last round that evening. Moving in bright and fast, Apollo caught Rocky flush on the jaw with the stuff champions are made of: guts, grit, and *gesundheit!* Rocky staggered; he was like a marathon dancer who had lost his partner sixty hours before, but was still leaning and moving as if there was someone there. Apollo cut loose with pure savagery. Rocky was driven against the ropes and received last rites in the form of a devastating beating from the champion . . . Rocky was dropped. He sat stunned in the middle of the ring—Raggedy Andy with the stuffing knocked out of him. Everything was distorted . . . he looked for a familiar face . . . where was someone to help him? Mickey, Mike and Al screamed frantically for him to stay down.

The referee was counting: ". . . six . . . seven . . . eight . . ." He got no further.

Insanely, Rocky got to his feet and tensed with renewed energy. He was a wounded, wild, animal. The tide had suddenly turned and washed Rocky up on Apollo Creed. Rocky dropped low and caught Apollo with a pair of terrific body punches that seemed to drive Apollo's diaphragm up to his throat. A loud crack was heard. A glaze of pain covered Apollo's eyes with the jellied aspic of cruel reality. It was only by a supreme effort that the champion stayed upright. He was so badly hurt that he began to bend in the middle, like storeaway furniture: Pretty soon, if he didn't rally, there'd be no room for him, and he'd be put away. Rocky kept coming; he imagined that Apollo was a frozen side of beef just waiting for Rocky to tenderize its dark flesh. But Apollo defrosted like a flash, flicked dread jabs into Rocky's eyes. Still, Rocky waded in with punches that seemed to bulge out Apollo's back. Creed took the punishment like a stoic. He had picked the Italian Stallion, and now that the horse was running wild, stampeding all over him, it was up to him to tame the wild beast or kill it in the name of sport. Blood, like dampened flame, or the soft tongue of the sanguinary soul, ran from Apollo's mouth. He didn't like losing it—blood was personal, his Universal O automotive fuel. In the clinch he leaned over Rocky, and it dripped down the Italian's neck and shoulders like a mantle. Apollo shielded his wound from the ringside judges and continued to fight.

At the end of the round, when the bell clanged and the red bulbs atop the ringposts lit up, Apollo's men rushed out and guided him to his corner.

". . . Ribs broke . . ." Apollo managed to say. Blood was still trickling from his mouth. The trainer felt his ribs.

"Yo' bleedin' inside, man. Get that doctor!"

"One more round," Apollo said. "Only one more round to go. I won't die."

"Who says you won't, Don't kill yourself, man. Let the doctor stop the fight."

"Stop jivin'!" Apollo replied. "Yo' talkin' to the champ."

The trainer, knowing Apollo had made up his mind, gave him the best advice he could under the circumstances. "Cover the ribs . . . look here, elbow down tight . . . tight! Stand straight . . . you're the best, you're the fuckin' best!"

"Thanks," Apollo replied.

Rocky was no longer recognizable. His face had been beaten to jelly, but his mood was buoyant. He, too, had that special something that only good fighters have—a false sense of invincibility, a mistaken macho interpretation of what life is all about, deadened nerve endings, and a round-trip, one-time ticket to fame and fortune.

"How I look out there, Mick?" he asked.

"Great, kid, great!" the worried Mickey replied. There was still a chance his man, Rocky, could go blind. Creed had been working on Rocky's already horribly marred eyes. It wasn't worth it; nothing was worth getting yourself a dog and a tin cup for. But that was one of the occupational hazards. The fight game was suicide for some, a better life for others. Benny "Kid" Paret had died, and six other young hopefuls had sprung up in his place, rubbing the resin from their gloves and snorting air through their nostrils before they had even begun to beat or to be beaten.

The doctor leaned over Rocky and checked his eyes.

"One more round. How do you feel?" he asked solicitously.

Rocky, approaching the supreme moment of his life, couldn't be bothered with pain or doctors. "Fine. Go away, I'm gonna make it!"

Everyone was distraught by Rocky's condition.

"We gotta stop it, kid," Mickey said softly.

"Ya gave it ya best shot!" Mike said.

"Nobody's gonna say ya didn't give ya' all. I can't let ya go out," Mickey declared.

Rocky stood and eyed them all. Hate filled him. His friends were trying to keep him from going all the way. He was determined to go the fifteen rounds, if he had to be dragged around the ring by a power mower or a human conveyor belt. "I'll kill ya all. Don't stop nothin'," he hissed quietly and in an impassioned manner—something like a snake that had just learned to talk.

The last round, and both contenders were in pain. Apollo moved cautiously out of his corner and circled to Rocky's right. The TV commentators stared unswervingly at the fighters: "The fight has slowed down to a near standstill . . . Creed circles to Rocky's right . . . The Spectrum is nearly silent . . . Neither fighter has made a motion to throw. I've never seen anything like it in the last round of a championship fight. Apollo spits blood on the canvas. It appears he is protecting his right side. His ribs were probably barbecued at the end of round fourteen . . . It's confirmed, unofficially, Creed's ribs may be broken . . . Apollo fakes a left and throws a big, tired right . . . Balboa's mouthpiece is out! Creed attacks with one hand!"

Apollo feinted and Rocky fell for it. The champion unleashed a lethal blow to the side of the head that jolted Rocky's mouthpiece into the second row. Rocky sagged against the ropes in a crucified position: Maybe that's what it was all about —martyrdom, suffering, ascension with the crown of thorns piercing through to heaven . . . only pain is holy. The crowd, insane with joy, cried out as one and leaped to their feet: "He's hurt! He's hurt!"

Rocky's bloody teeth were exposed to Apollo in a snarl as he waved him to come ahead and fight toe to toe. Apollo obliged with a weary but effective burst of rights and lefts that had kayo written on every punch. Rocky countered the assault blow for blow.

Rocky exploded, "Gimme ya' best!!"

Mickey looked at the clock: TEN SECONDS TO GO.

Even louder, Rocky shouted again, "GIMME YA' BEST!!"

Blood sprayed over the ropes and onto the ringside photographers; they were horrified and wiped away the blood. The fighters stood toe to toe and dragged every bit of strength from their souls and beat each other without mercy. Hypnotized, they entered a dimension far beyond blood and pain. The minutes went by: SIX, FIVE, FOUR, THREE, TWO, ONE! And the last bell stopped the action. The arena exploded with thunderous approval, it had gotten all it wanted: viciousness, violence, brutality, everything short of death. Their cornermen rushed to the collapsed fighters. In the midst of all the confusion, both fighters looked at each other with unabashed respect. It was sentimental and kind of stupid—or do you always love the one you hate, or kill the one you love for a fee? Balboa and Creed stood like blood-drenched gladiators on the most dramatic night of their lives. As though reacting to some unspoken command, they stepped toward one another and embraced. Apollo whispered in Rocky's ear, "Ain't gonna be no rematch."

"Don't want none," Rocky answered.

Mickey separated them and led Rocky back to his corner. He embraced him in a huge, fatherly embrace. Suddenly Rocky felt tired.

The announcer entered the ring. The microphones were lowered, and he spoke into them: "Attention, please! Attention! Ladies and gentlemen, tonight we have had the rare privilege of witnessing the greatest exhibition of stamina and guts ever in the history of sports."

The crowd went wild again and stamped,

roared, bounced chairs up and down, unable to contain its own repressed energy.

The announcer continued: "Ladies and gentle-men, we have a split decision!"

Apollo didn't expect this, and tensed. His cor-ner nervously tried to reassure him. It did no good.

Rocky didn't expect it either, and looked in confusion at Mickey, but Mickey was frozen with anticipation.

"Judge Walker scores it eight-seven, Creed. Judge Roseman scores it eight-seven, Balboa," continued the announcer.

Apollo was rigid. His eyes radiated fear. To lose the crown on this night, after the fight he fought, would really kill him. A silence blanketed the arena.

"Judge Conners scores it nine-six, Creed. Win-ner and still heavyweight champion of the world, Apollo Creed!"

Rocky forced himself to smile; it hurt real bad. He looked out at the waves of cheering fans that circled the ring and reached out toward him. Mickey grabbed Rocky's hand and raised it.

"I don't care what they say, you're a winner," Mickey said to him.

"Yo, can I have my locker back?" kidded Rocky.

The two men looked at each other and grinned. Mickey hugged Rocky like a son. He raised Rocky's hand again. Rocky turned away from Mickey and patted Al on the shoulder. Al smiled wearily. Rocky stared across the ring at Apollo Creed, who stood victorious but physically broken. Once again the two men locked stares that spoke of the admiration they felt for each other. He climbed out of the ring, and the fans crushed forward screaming his name, as if the sound of it would give each of them a little piece of him for them to take home. They were still waving those red, white, and blue banners they had bought outside and come in with.

Rocky also climbed out of the ring, pulling the blue velvet ropes apart like ribs that protect the heart; he was moving toward the beating, toward the muscle that made the whole place jump with excitement—the people. Waves of them, his fans, surged forward. Mickey became apprehensive as they advanced, knocking each other over and screaming as they came. They shoved the police aside and clutched the air.

As Creed came down the aisle, his army of bodyguards swung angrily at the crowd, but they were soon engulfed by screaming waves of humanity. Suddenly, the waves lifted Apollo high above them and carried him along, pressing his body past a tumultuous sea of hands. He floated above legions of these undulating finger-creatures, fearful that he would be dropped and crushed on the floor below.

On the opposite aisle, Rocky experienced the same overwhelming adulation by his fans, but he wasn't frightened by it, not the way Apollo was. Mickey tried his best to control things, but his voice was drowned out in the growing clamor. The fans shoved the guards aside and hoisted Rocky to their shoulders, far above the madding crowd.

Rocky's and Creed's fans were aggressively competing against each other, chanting, *"Creed, Creed, Creed,"* while Rocky's fans countered by

bellowing, *"Rocky, Rocky, Rocky!"* It was an im-
promptu choral work that would have pleased
the most far-our composer. Paulie tried to get to
Rocky but was shoved aside, and he started swinging. His versatile leisure suit, which he wore with
a color-coordinated open sport shirt and matching trouser slightly flared at the bottom, got
mussed up.

Both Rocky and Apollo were completely at the
mercy of the crowd. They were being passed overhead and remained helpless as their bodies floated
up the aisle on the sea of hands. The chanting was
deafening.

Fearful that Rocky was in danger, Adrian tried
to move forward. Running headlong into the
crowd, she angled through the mass to get to
Rocky. Although she was manhandled and shoved
in a multitude of directions, she kept her feet.

She could see Rocky in the distance, being
borne toward her at the head of a procession. The
procession approached and passed Adrian. She
jumped to her toes and waved frantically to him,
but he didn't see her. She screamed Rocky's name
but wasn't heard at first; then somehow the deli-
cate voice lightly knifed through the racket and
reached Rocky. He looked in all directions, unable to locate Adrian. Finally he managed to see
her; she was jumping up and down and waving.
He tried to lower himself, but the crowd wouldn't
permit it. They were carrying him away.

In desperation, Rocky turned and began
climbing across people's heads and shoulders. He
resembled a man trying to go up on a down es-
calator. People were jammed so tightly together
that they made a solid floor of heads and shoul-

ders, a flat and bumpy rug of hair. Rocky managed to crawl across them to Adrian.

Still suspended in air, Rocky leaned down, and Adrian jumped up: They locked in an embrace.

"I love you . . . I love you . . . I love you . . ." was all Adrian could say. It was all she had to say. It was all he wanted to hear.

The two lovers, clinging to one another, were swept along into the greatest night anyone could ever remember.